STORY ONE

Adopt a GLURB!

I'm cute!

HERE'S THE GLURB

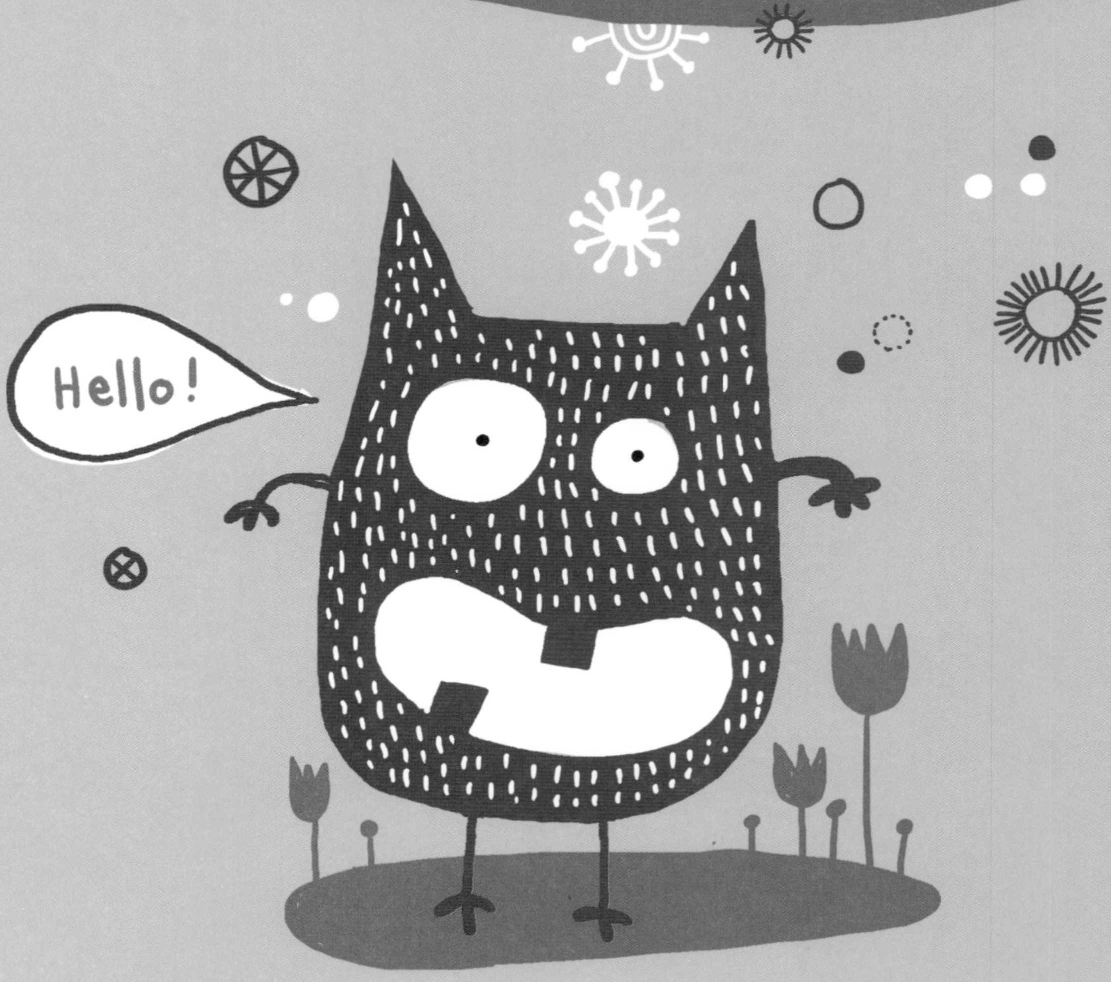
Hello!

The glurb is a cute little monster that you can keep at home with you, just like a dog or a cat.

THE glurb IS VERY FUNNY.

If you don't take good care of him, you'll be in trouble. He's a little RASCAL.

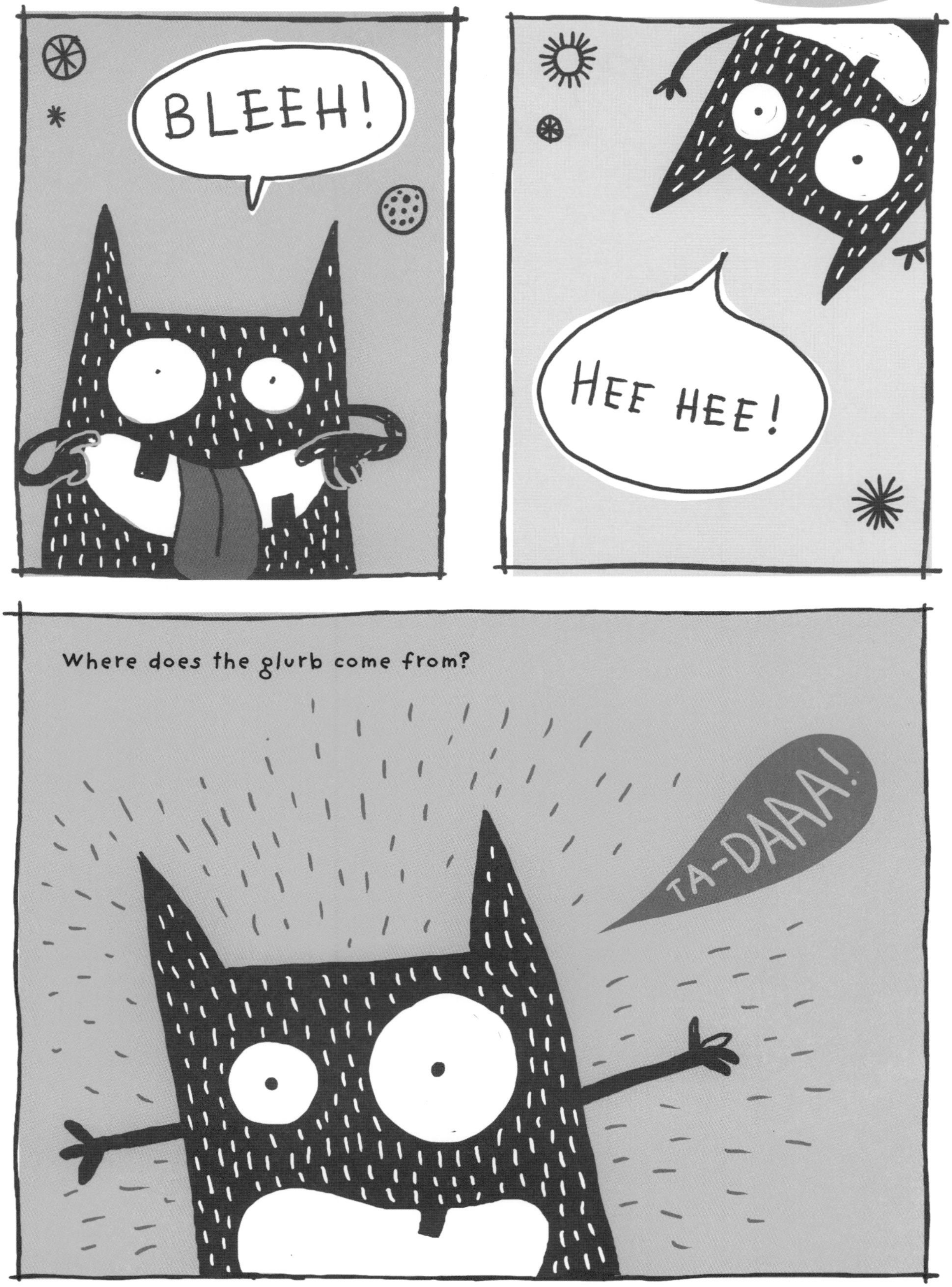
BLEEH!
HEE HEE!
Where does the glurb come from?
TA-DAAA!

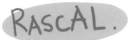

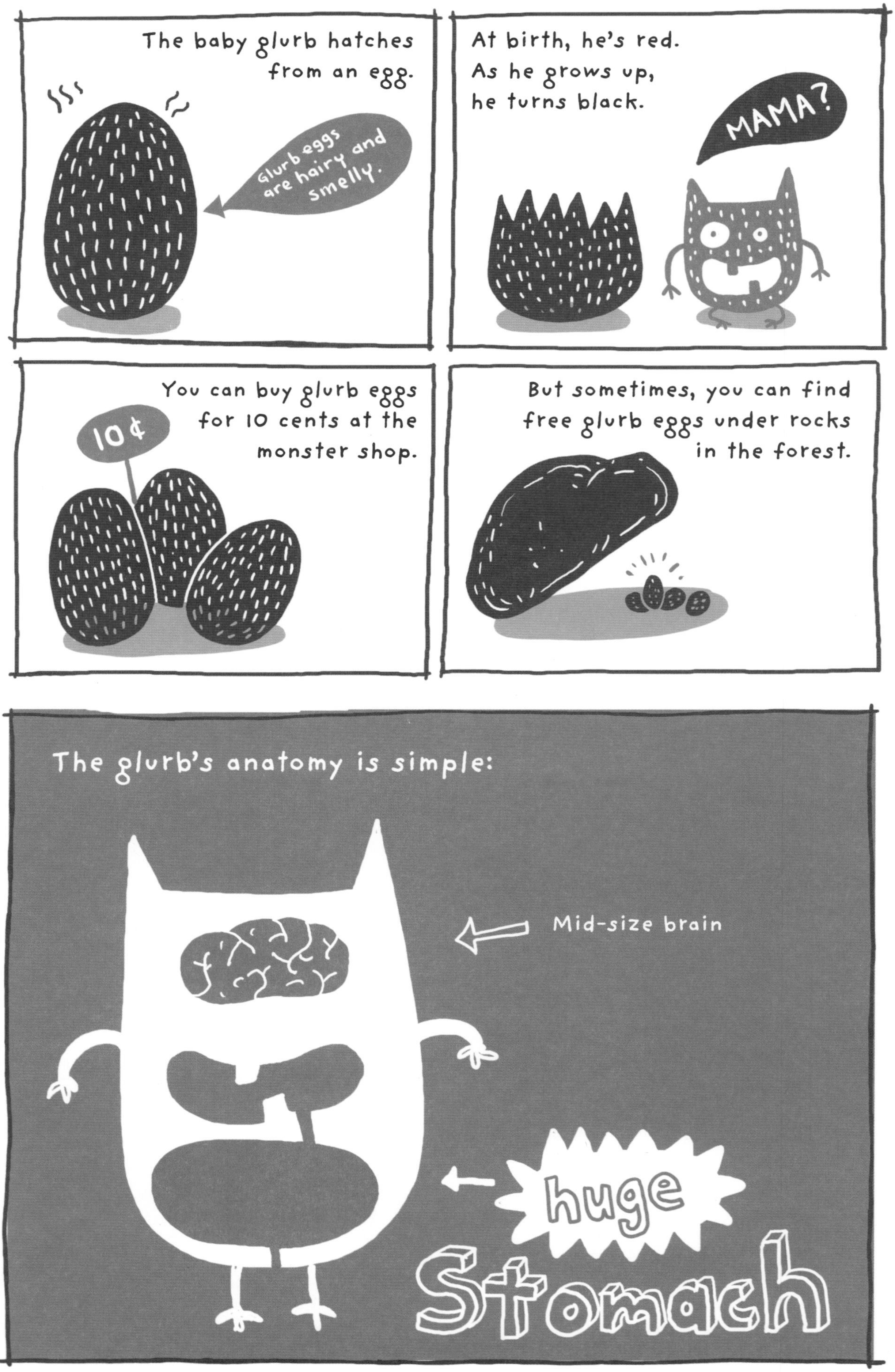
The baby glurb hatches from an egg.
Glurb eggs are hairy and smelly.
At birth, he's red. As he grows up, he turns black.
MAMA?
You can buy glurb eggs for 10 cents at the monster shop.
10¢
But sometimes, you can find free glurb eggs under rocks in the forest.
The glurb's anatomy is simple:
Mid-size brain
huge
Stomach

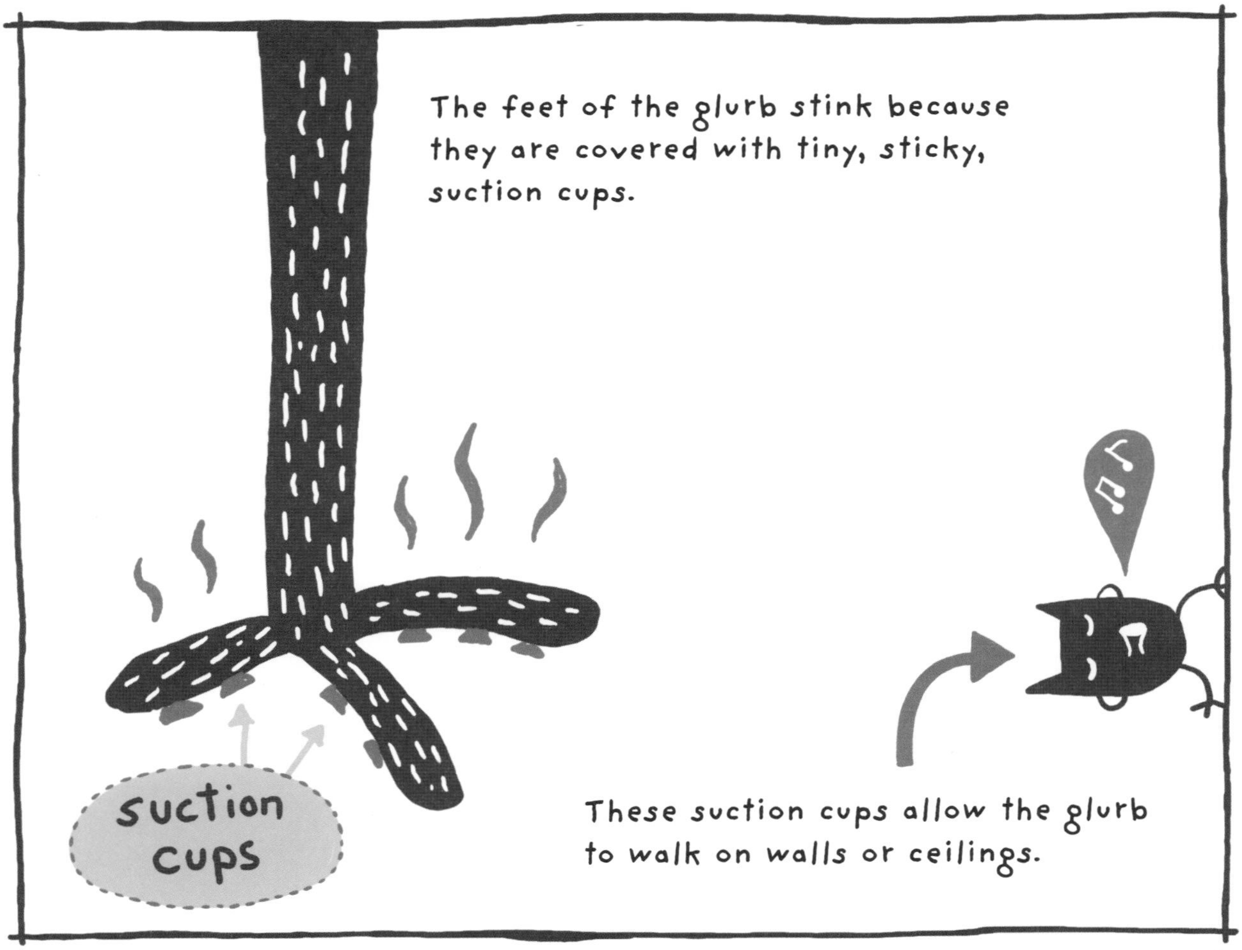
The feet of the glurb stink because they are covered with tiny, sticky, suction cups.
suction cups
These suction cups allow the glurb to walk on walls or ceilings.

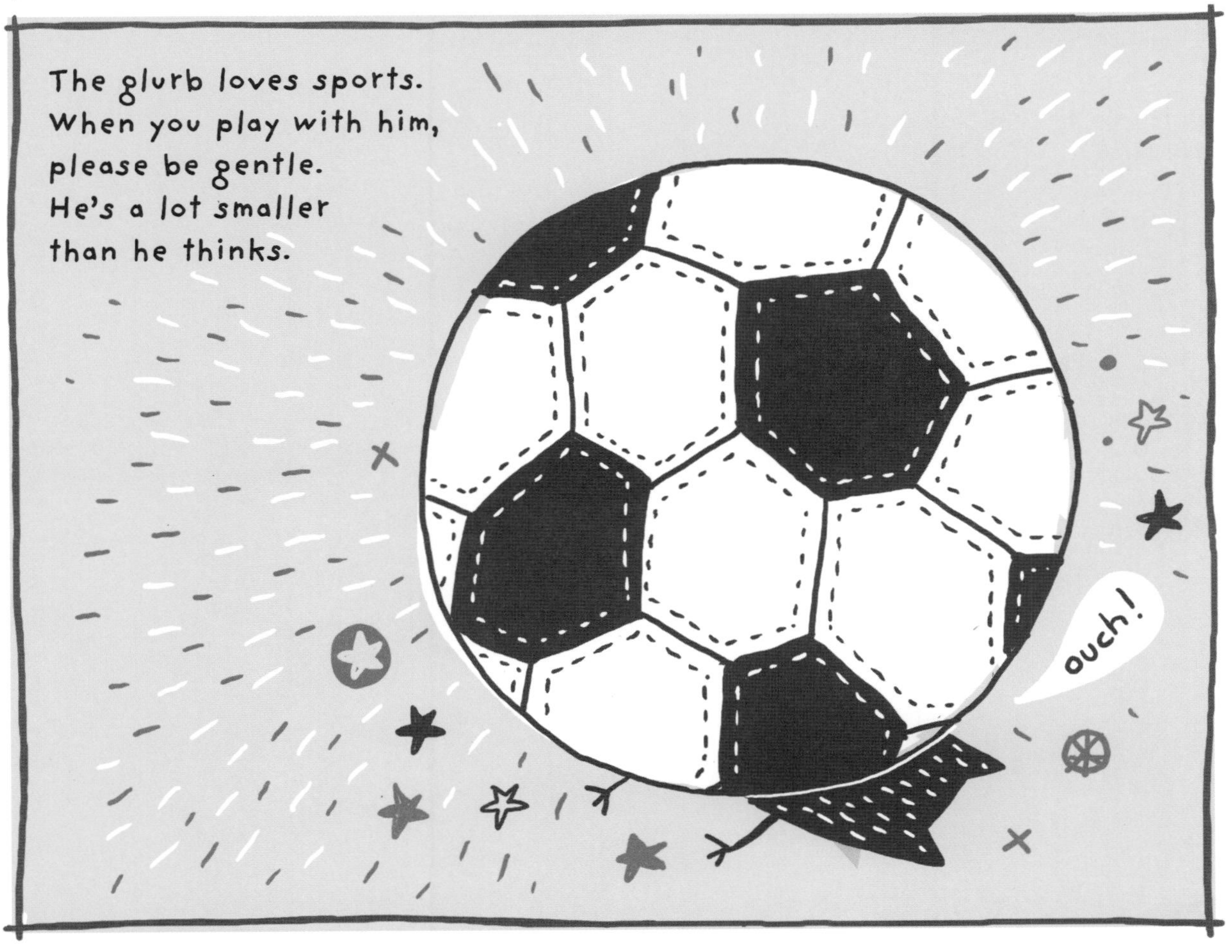
The glurb loves sports. When you play with him, please be gentle. He's a lot smaller than he thinks.
ouch!

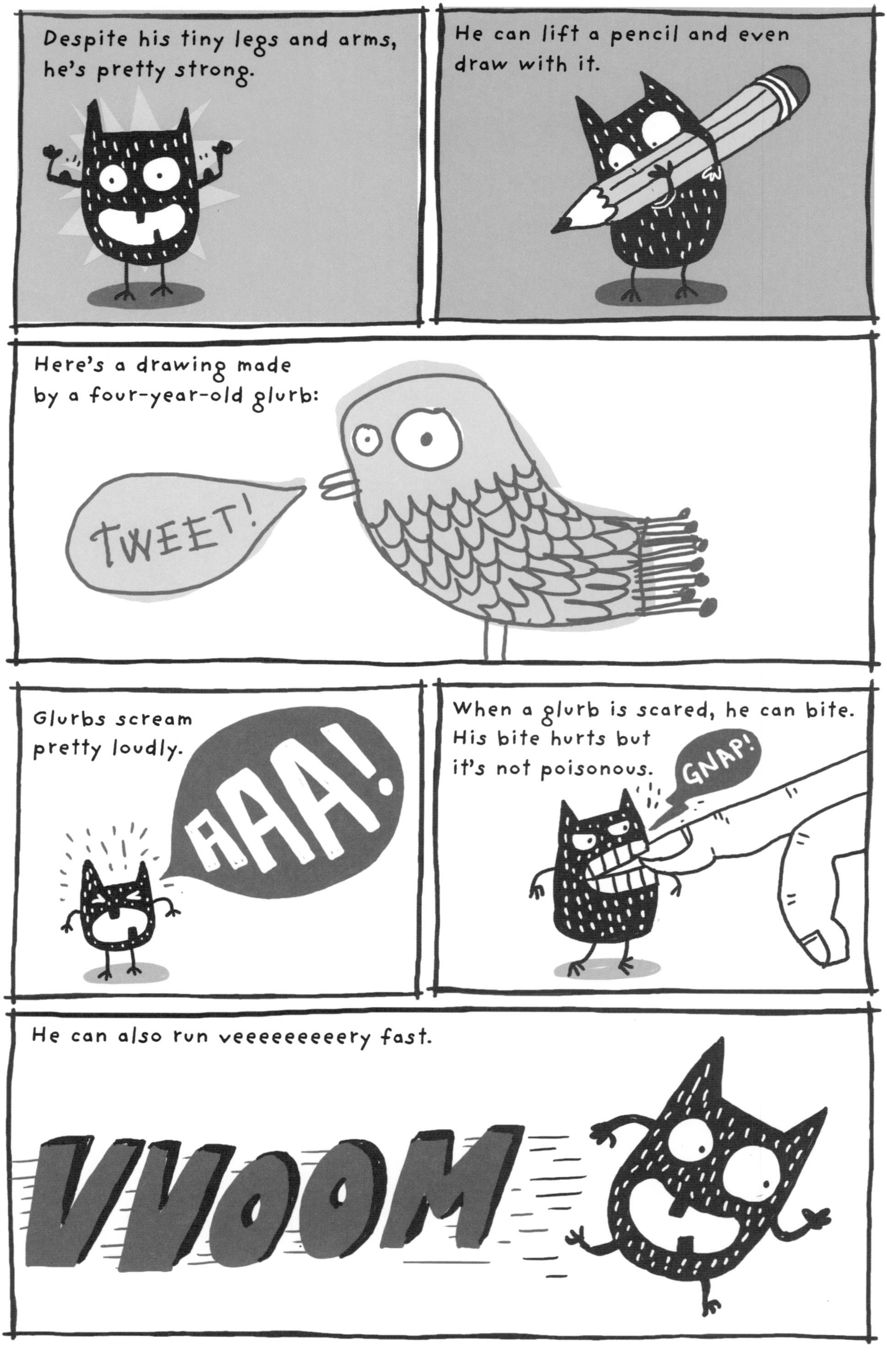

Despite his tiny legs and arms, he's pretty strong.
He can lift a pencil and even draw with it.
Here's a drawing made by a four-year-old glurb:
TWEET!
Glurbs scream pretty loudly.
AAA!
When a glurb is scared, he can bite. His bite hurts but it's not poisonous.
GNAP!
He can also run veeeeeeeeery fast.
VVOOM

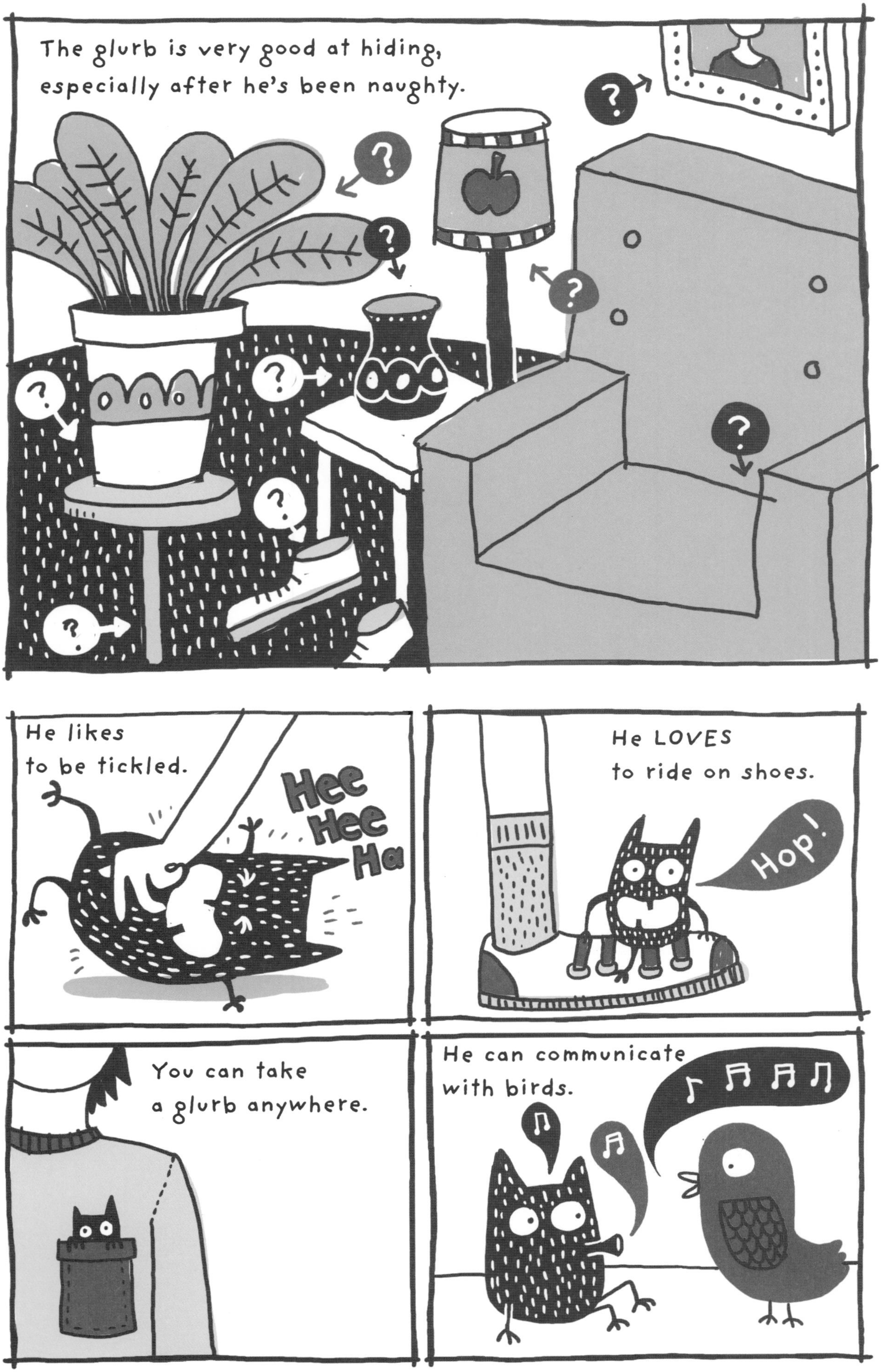
The glurb is very good at hiding, especially after he's been naughty.
He likes to be tickled.
Hee Hee Ha
He LOVES to ride on shoes.
Hop!
You can take a glurb anywhere.
He can communicate with birds.

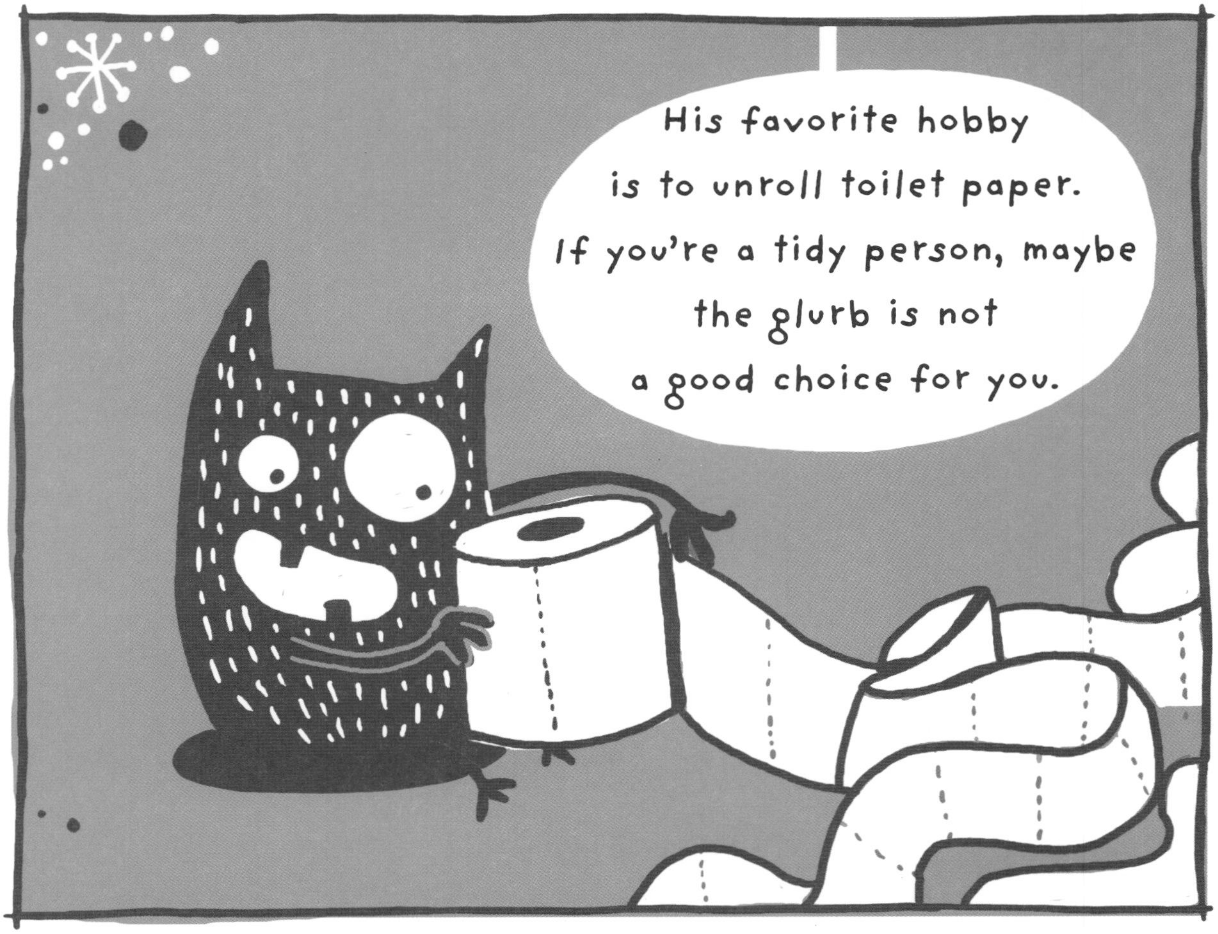
His favorite hobby is to unroll toilet paper. If you're a tidy person, maybe the glurb is not a good choice for you.

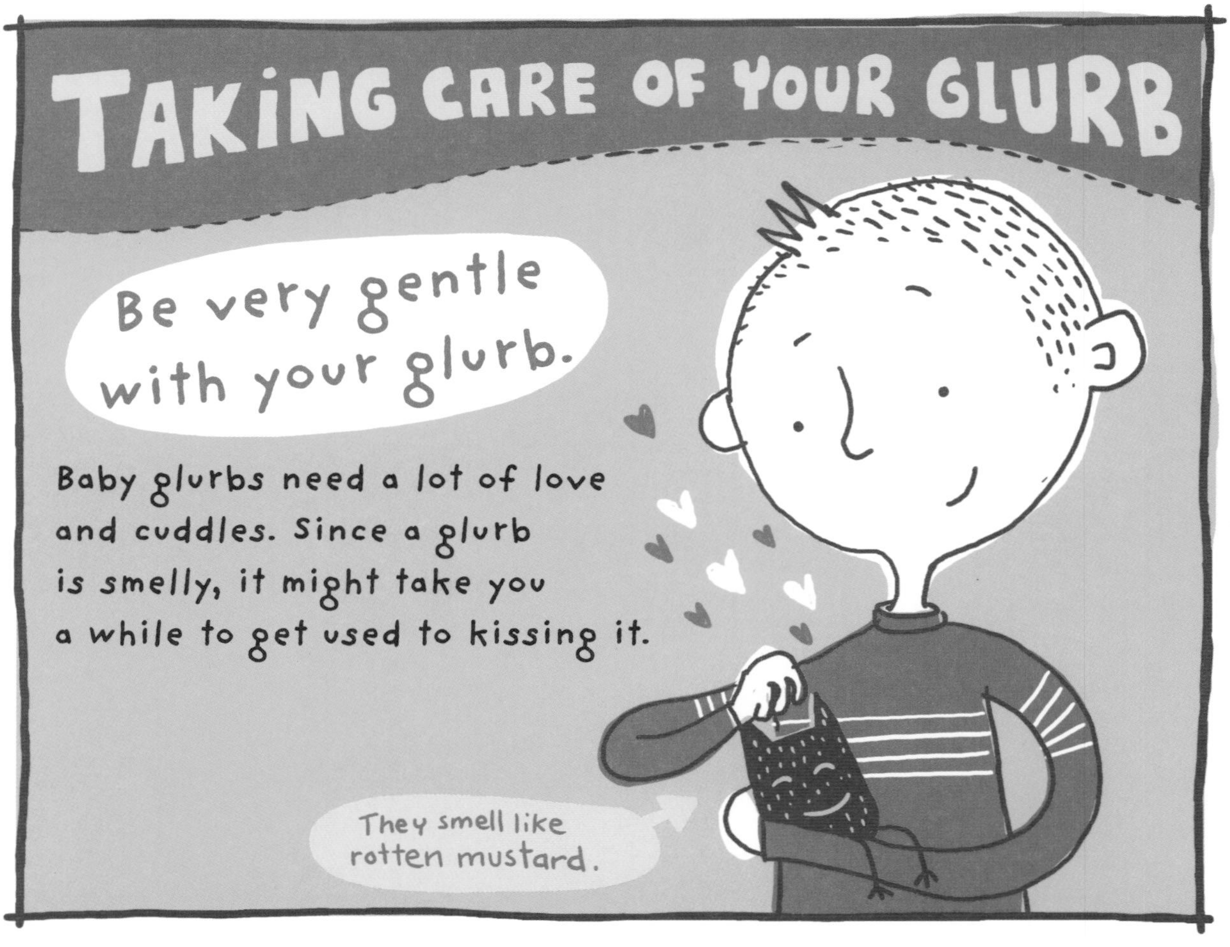
TAKING CARE OF YOUR GLURB
Be very gentle with your glurb.
Baby glurbs need a lot of love and cuddles. Since a glurb is smelly, it might take you a while to get used to kissing it.
They smell like rotten mustard.

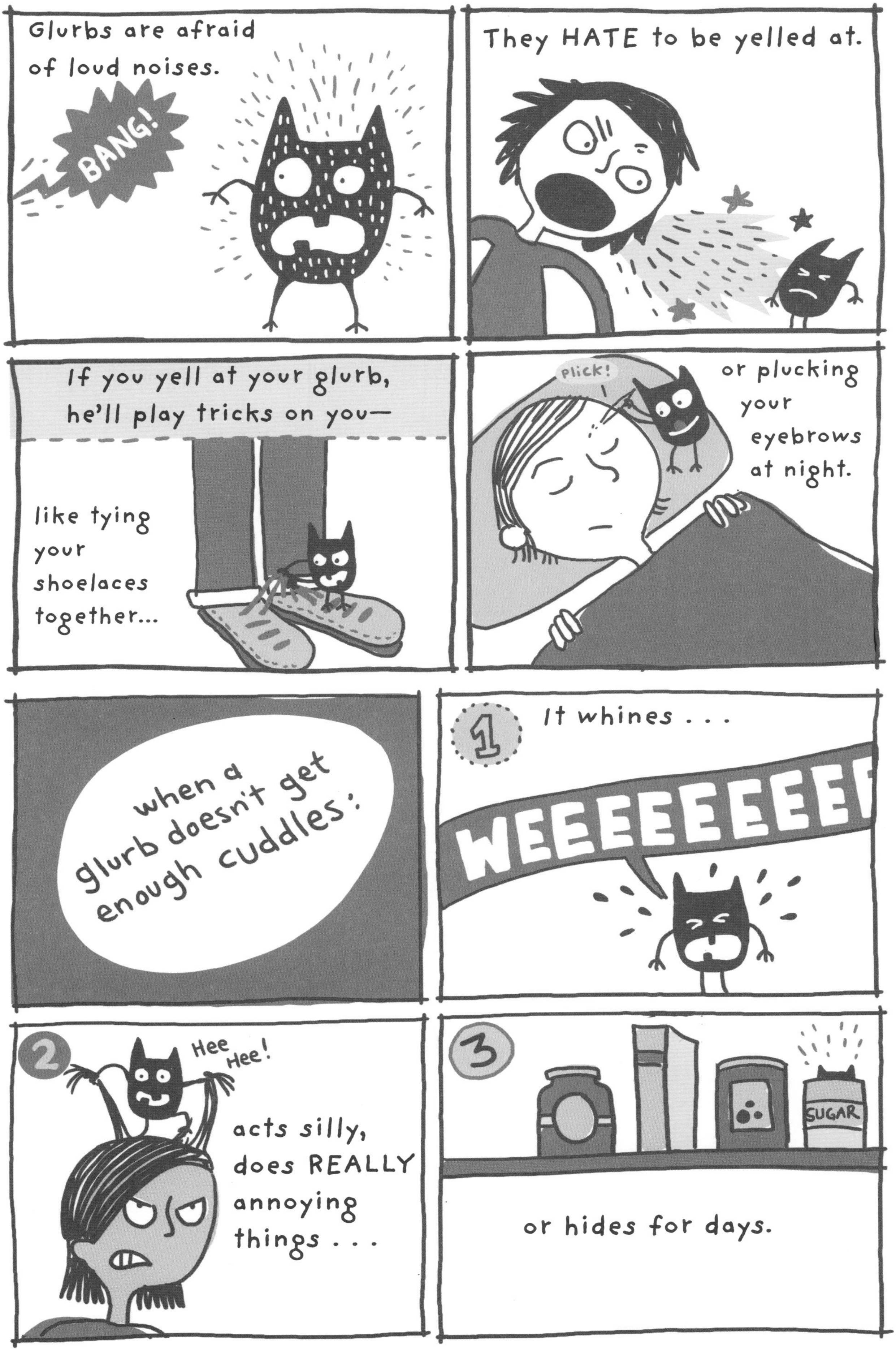

Glurbs are afraid of loud noises.
BANG!
They HATE to be yelled at.
If you yell at your glurb, he'll play tricks on you—
like tying your shoelaces together...
or plucking your eyebrows at night.
PLICK!
when a glurb doesn't get enough cuddles:
1
It whines . . .
WEEEEEEEEEE
2
Hee Hee!
acts silly, does REALLY annoying things . . .
3
SUGAR
or hides for days.

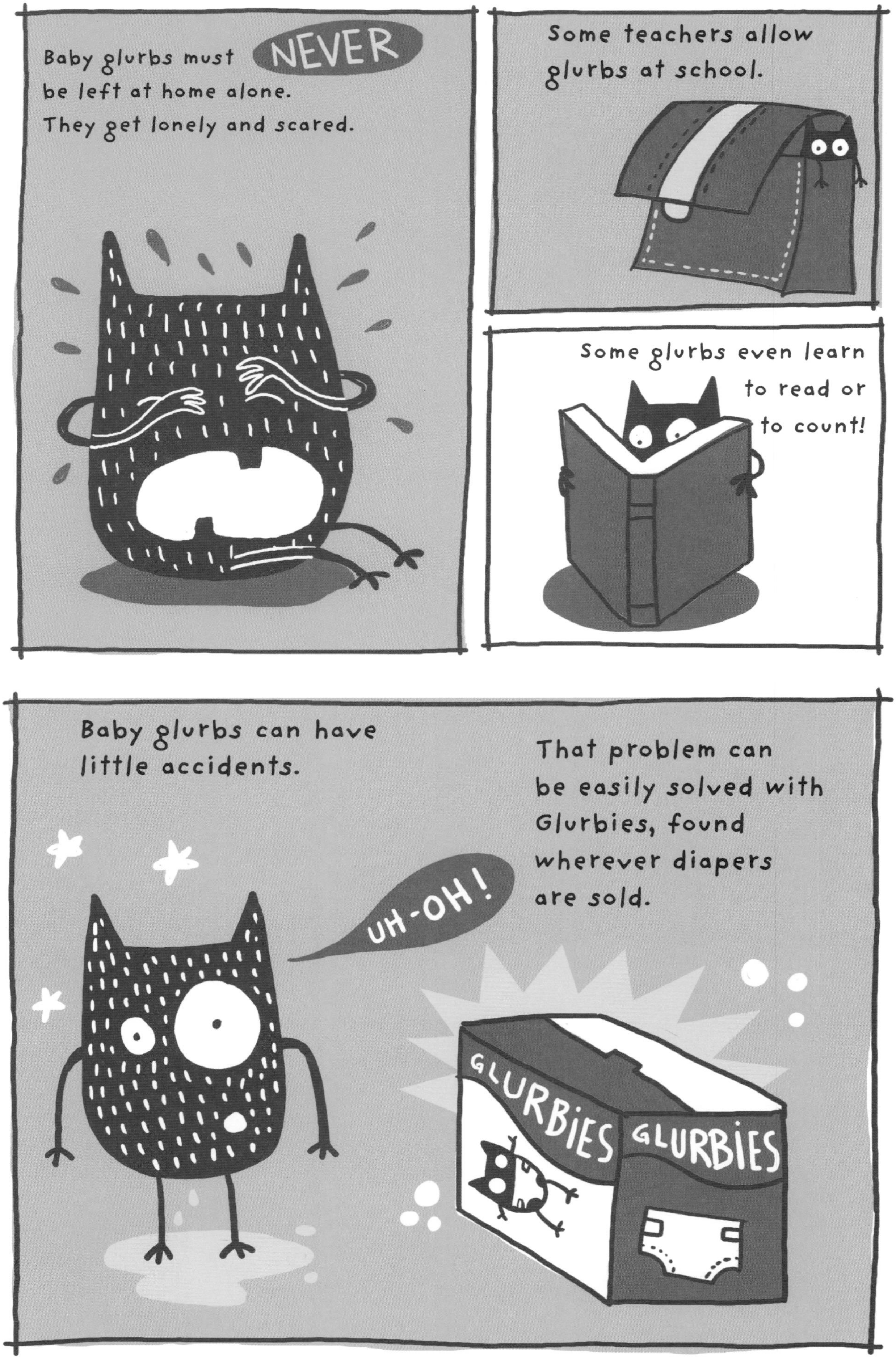
Baby glurbs must NEVER be left at home alone. They get lonely and scared.
Some teachers allow glurbs at school.
Some glurbs even learn to read or to count!
Baby glurbs can have little accidents.
UH-OH!
That problem can be easily solved with Glurbies, found wherever diapers are sold.
GLURBIES
GLURBIES

Keep your glurb CLEAN

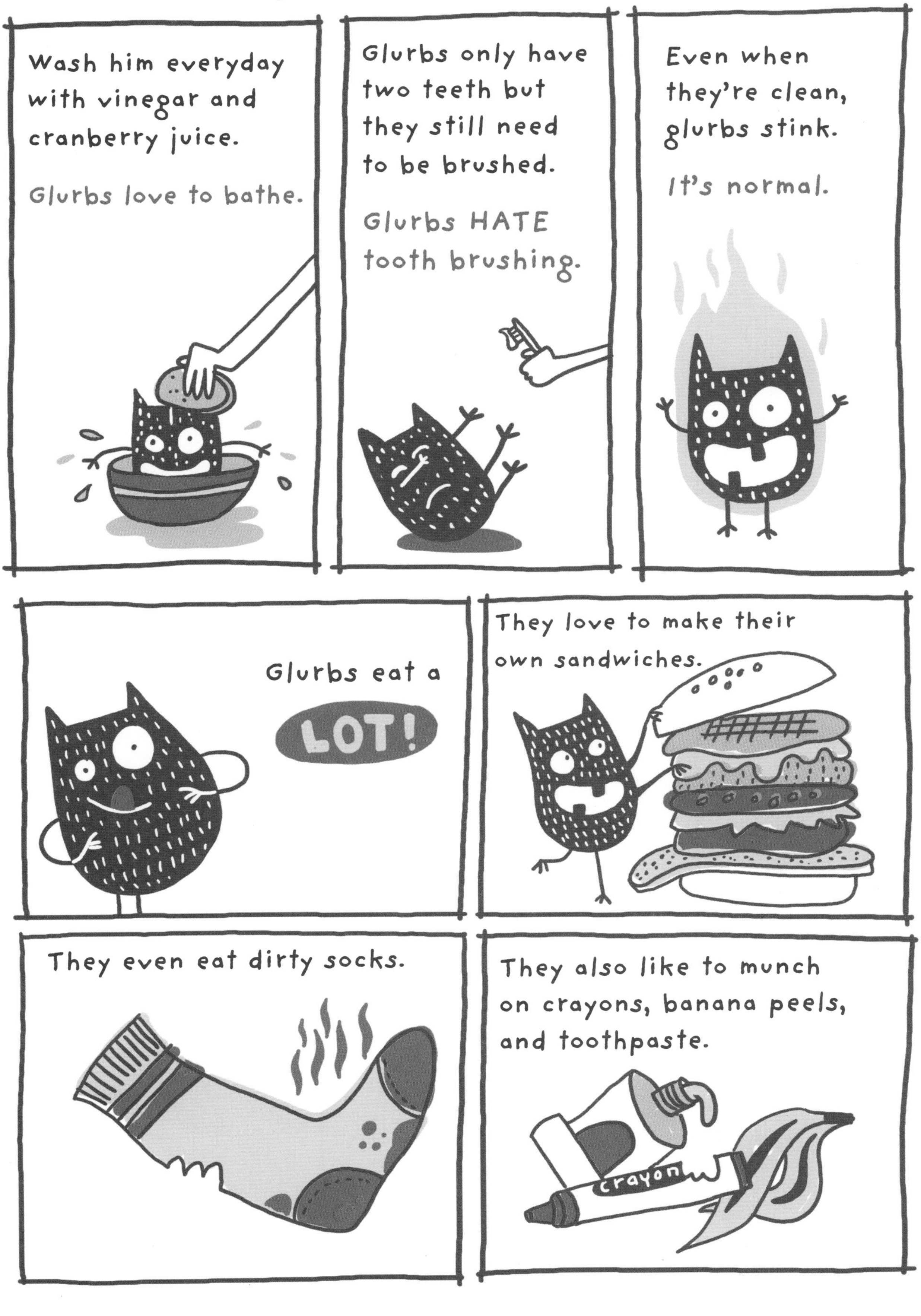

Wash him everyday with vinegar and cranberry juice.
Glurbs love to bathe.
Glurbs only have two teeth but they still need to be brushed.
Glurbs HATE tooth brushing.
Even when they're clean, glurbs stink.
It's normal.
Glurbs eat a
LOT!
They love to make their own sandwiches.
They even eat dirty socks.
They also like to munch on crayons, banana peels, and toothpaste.
crayon

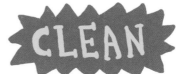

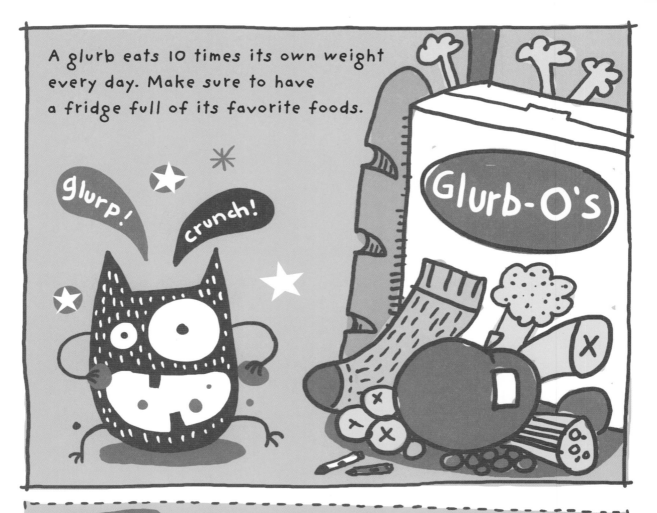

A glurb eats 10 times its own weight every day. Make sure to have a fridge full of its favorite foods.

glurp!
crunch!
Glurb-O's

ACTIVITIES TO KEEP YOUR GLURB HAPPY

1 GOO

Glurbs love everything gooey: wet play-dough, mashed bananas, melting jell-o.

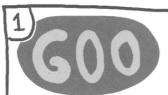

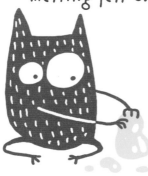

2 MUSIC

They LOVE music, especially jazz. They're also good dancers.

Doo-wop ba doo wah!

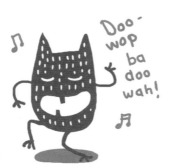

3 SLUG-RAISING

Glurbs like to play with slugs and slugs like to play with glurbs.

Heel!

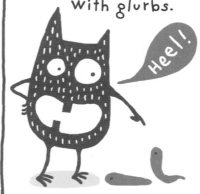

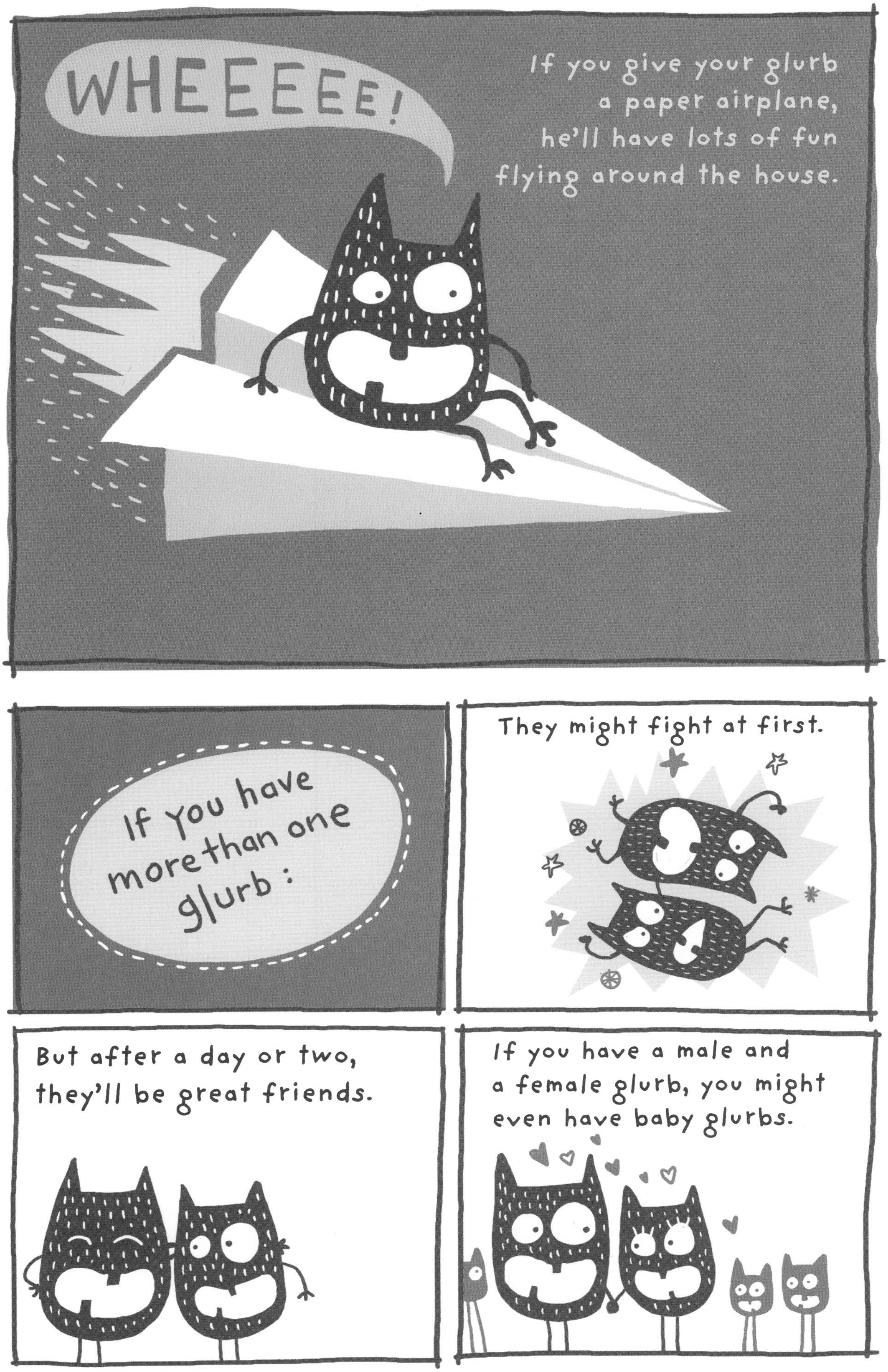
WHEEEEE!
If you give your glurb a paper airplane, he'll have lots of fun flying around the house.
If you have more than one glurb :
They might fight at first.
But after a day or two, they'll be great friends.
If you have a male and a female glurb, you might even have baby glurbs.

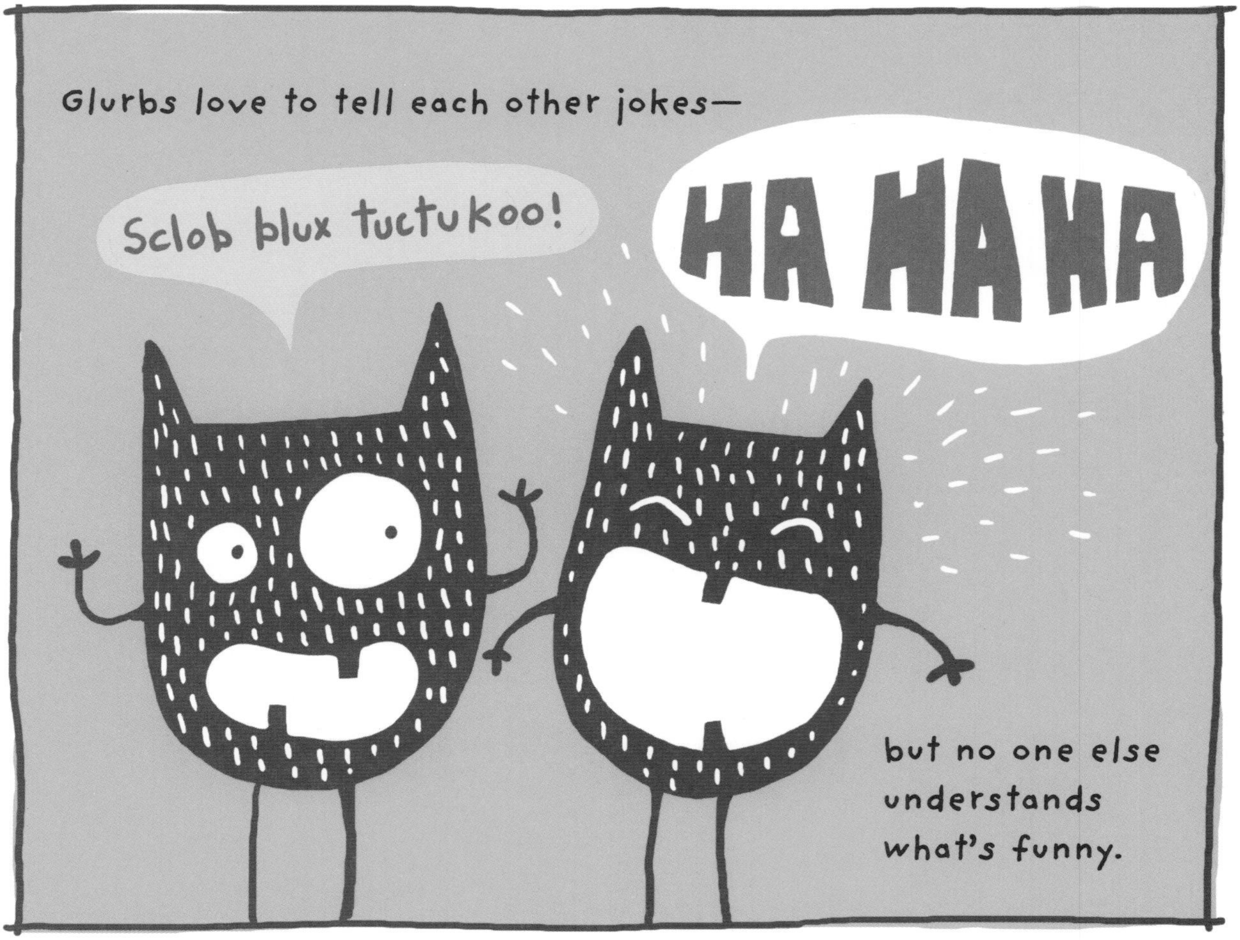
Glurbs love to tell each other jokes—
Sclob blux tuctukoo!
HA HA HA
but no one else understands what's funny.

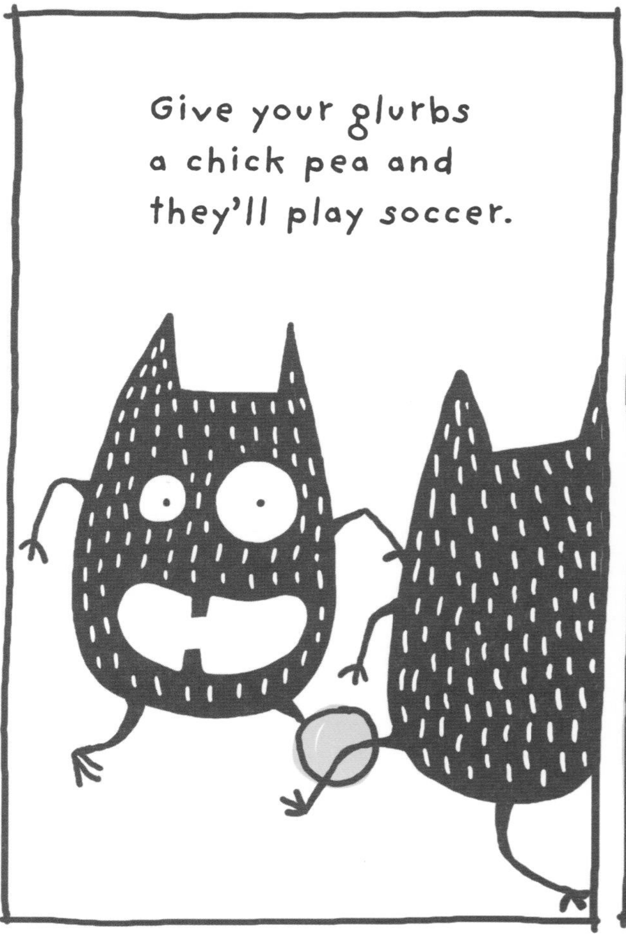
Give your glurbs a chick pea and they'll play soccer.

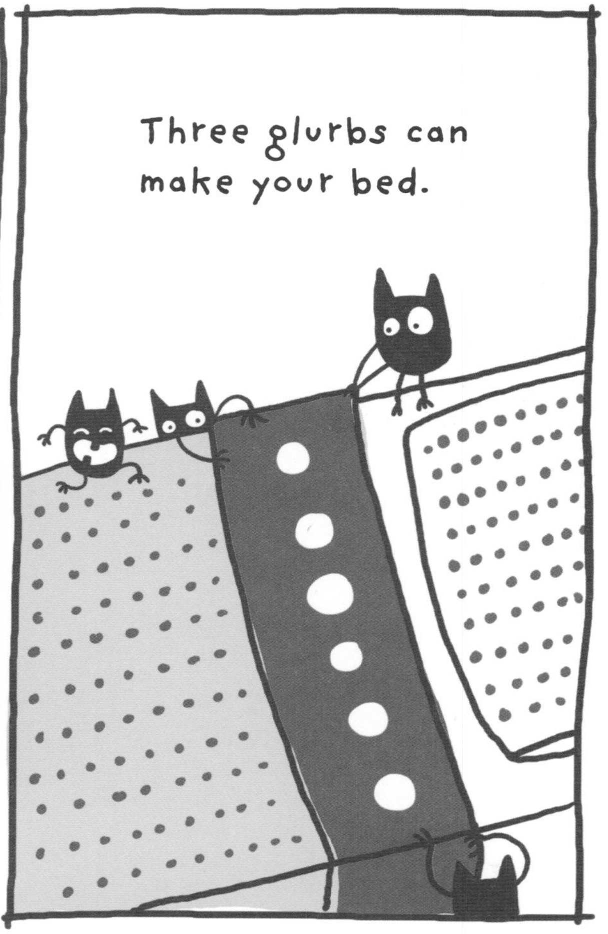
Three glurbs can make your bed.

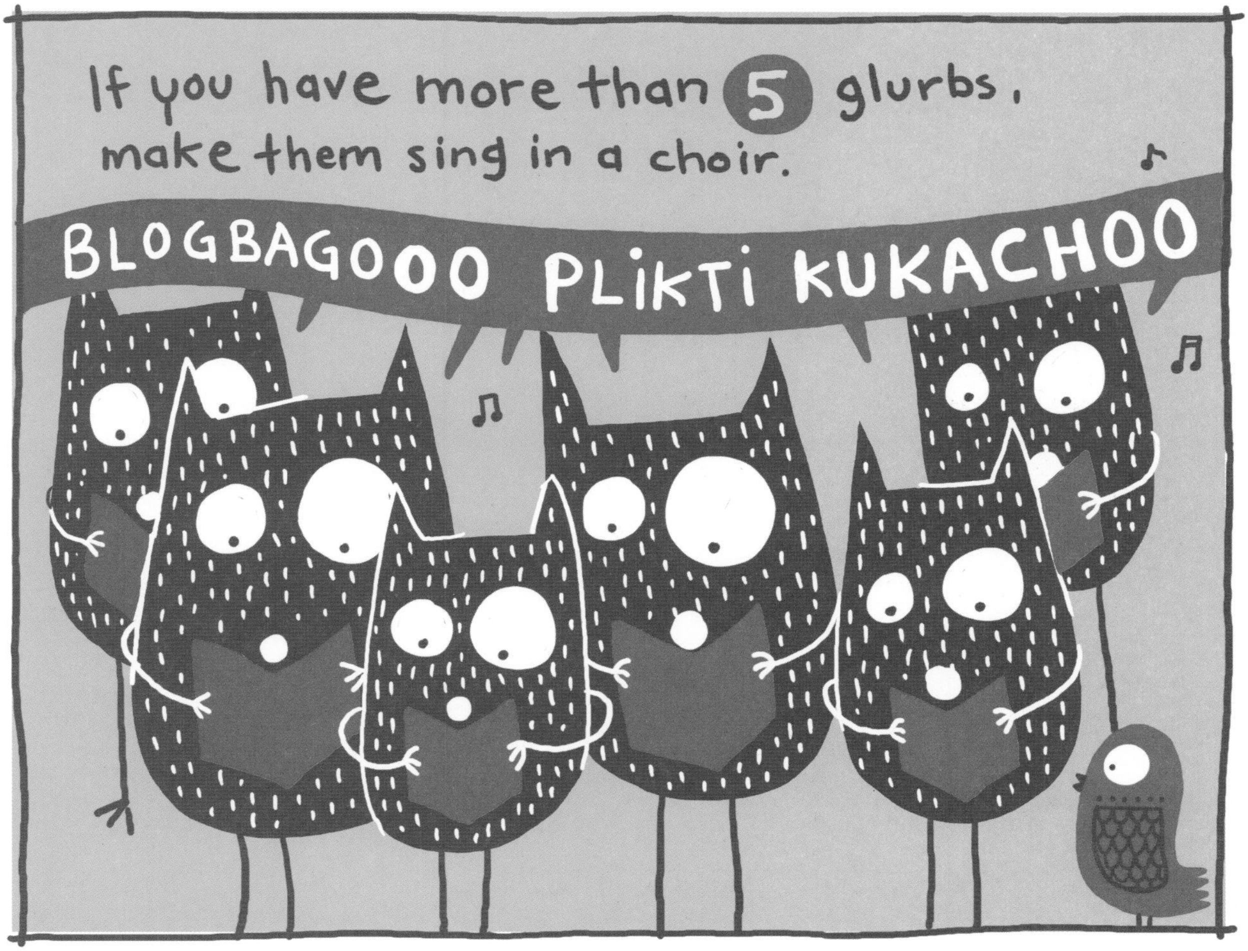
If you have more than 5 glurbs, make them sing in a choir.
BLOGBAGOOO PLIKTI KUKACHOO

Of course, if you have many glurbs, you'll need:

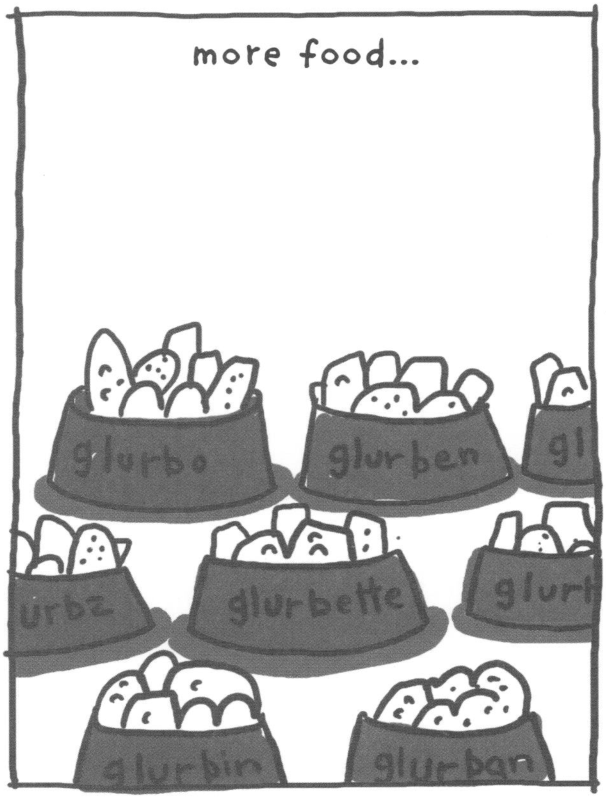
more food...
glurbo
glurben
glurbette
glurbin
glurban

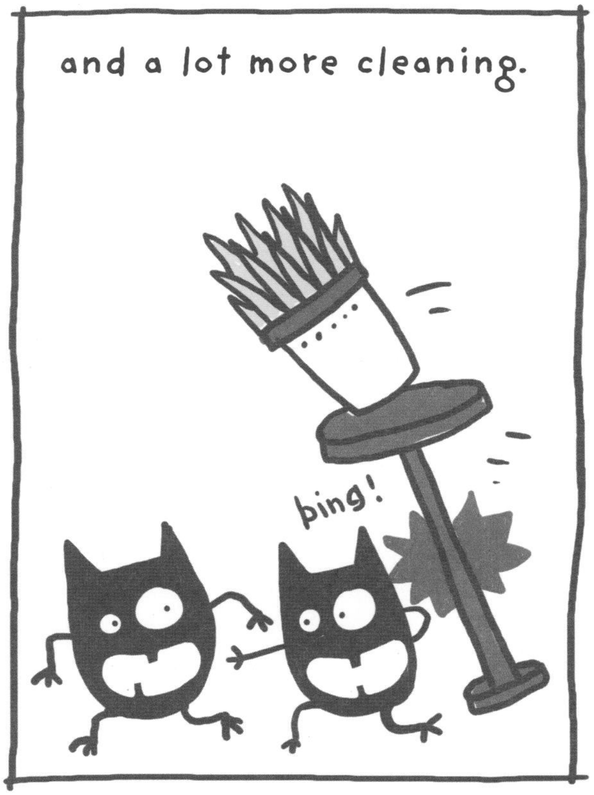
and a lot more cleaning.
bing!

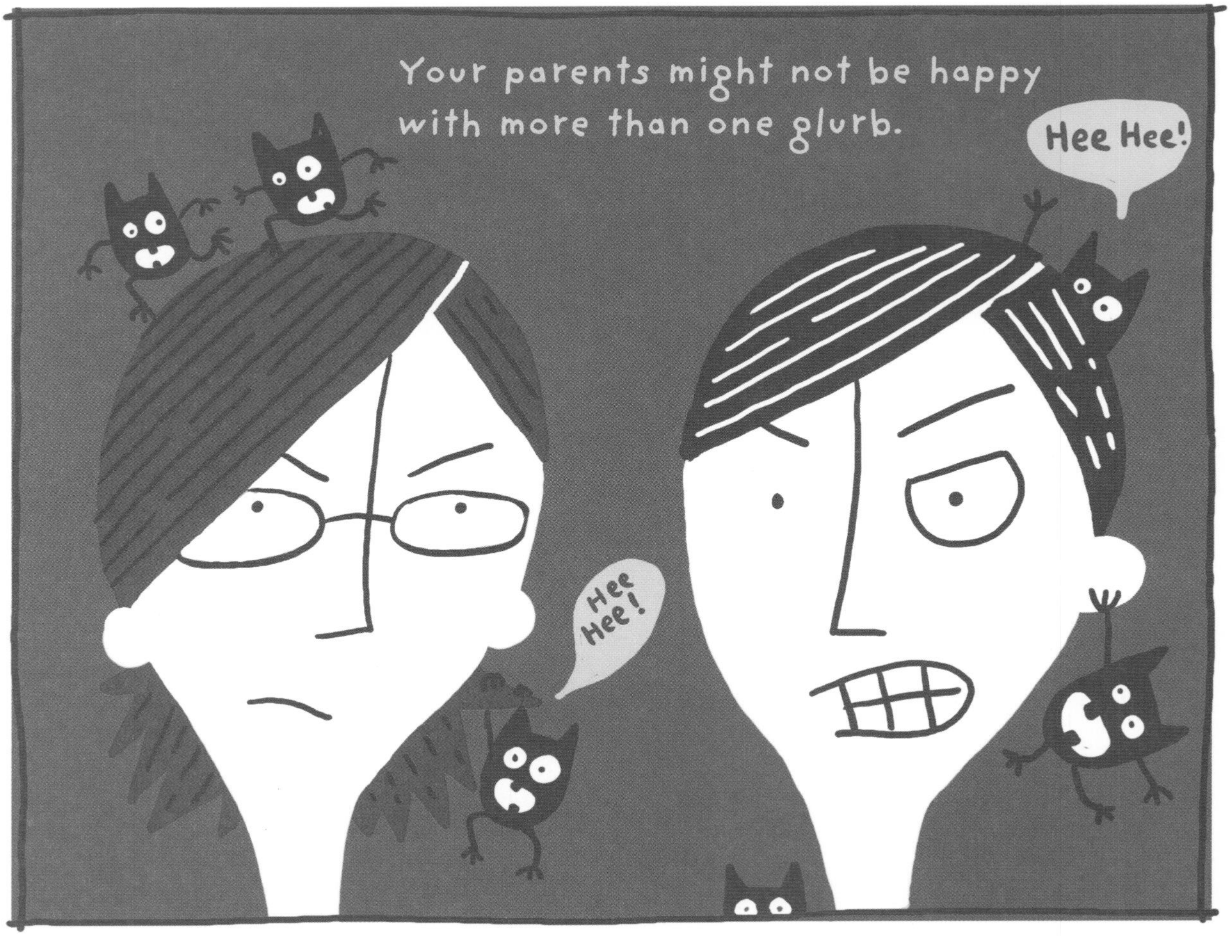
Your parents might not be happy
with more than one glurb.
Hee Hee!
Hee Hee!

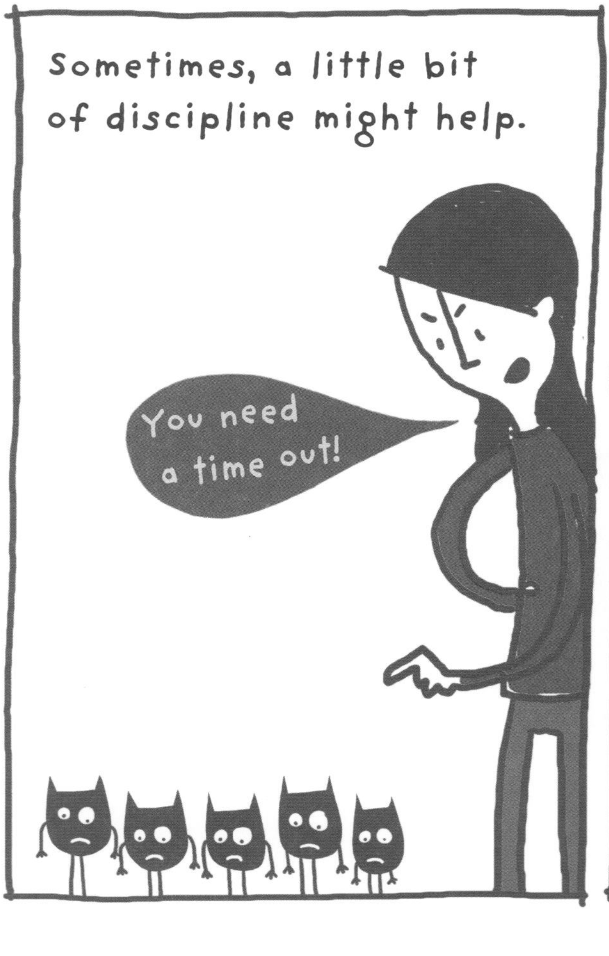
Sometimes, a little bit
of discipline might help.
You need a time out!

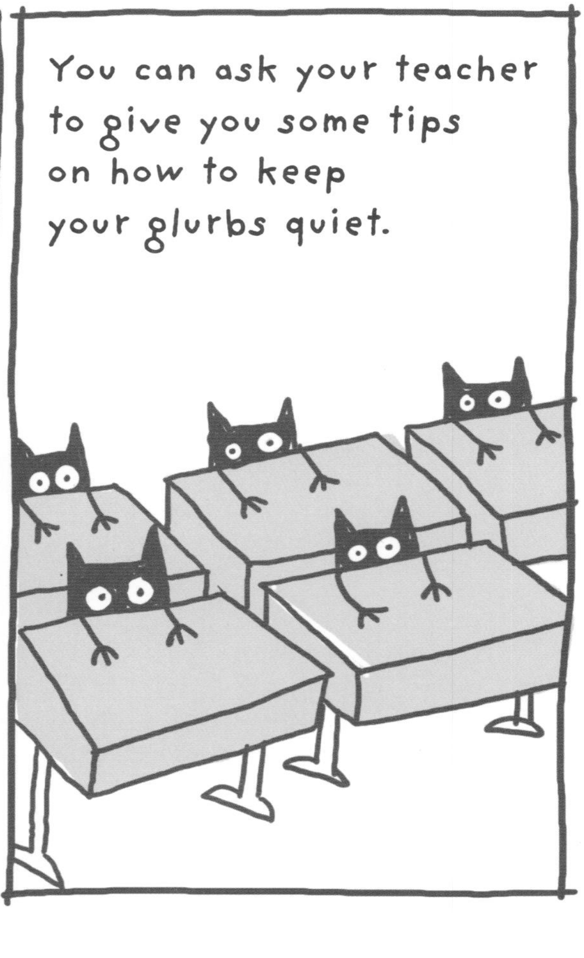
You can ask your teacher
to give you some tips
on how to keep
your glurbs quiet.

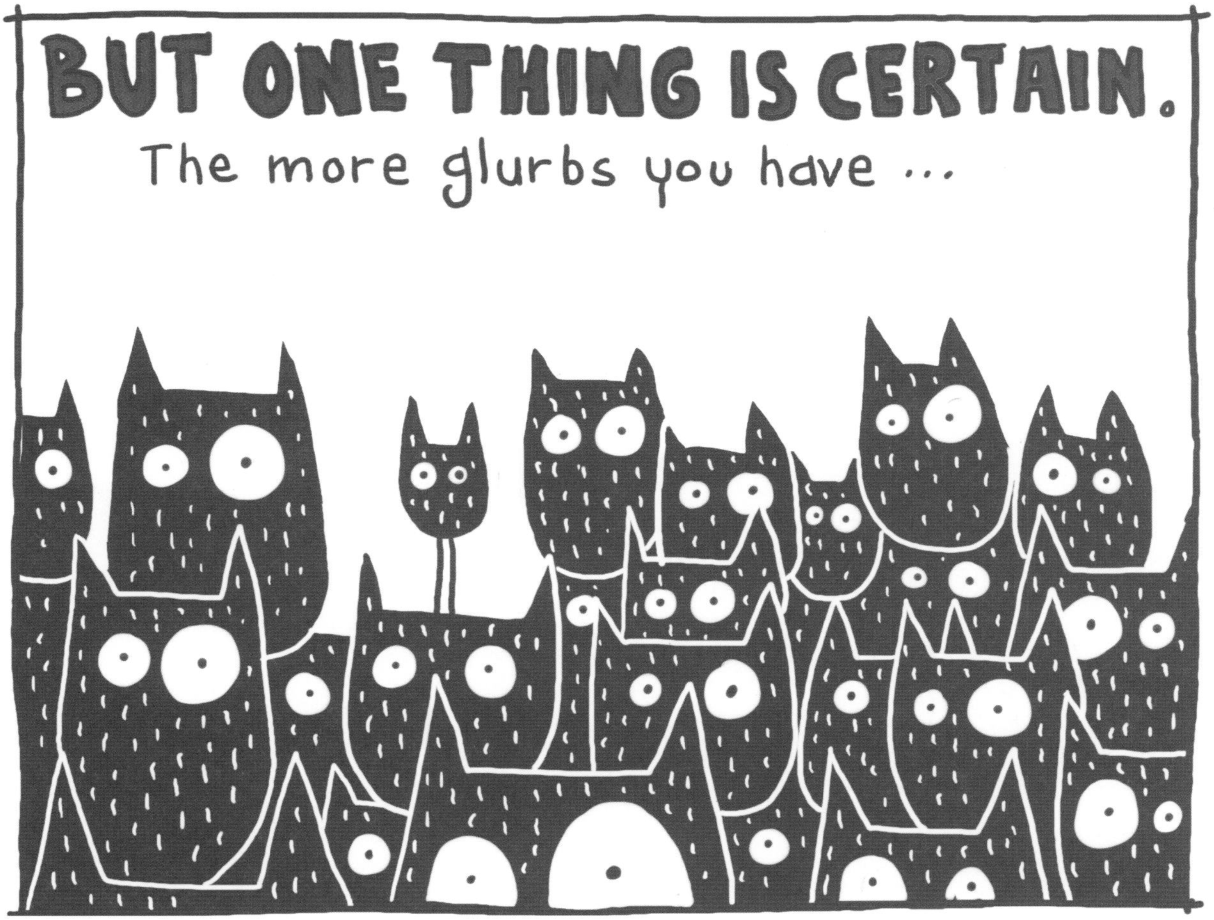
BUT ONE THING IS CERTAIN.
The more glurbs you have ...

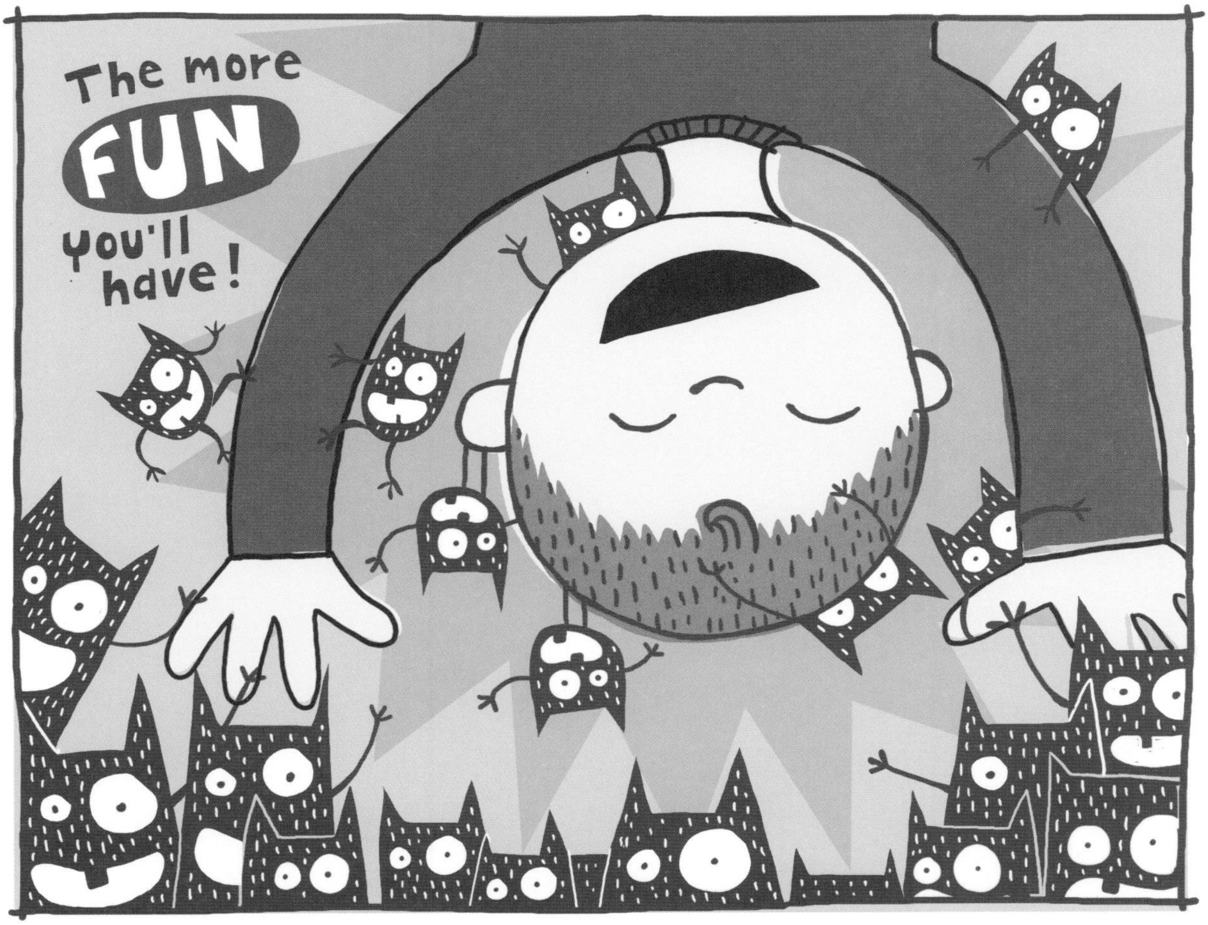
The more FUN you'll have!

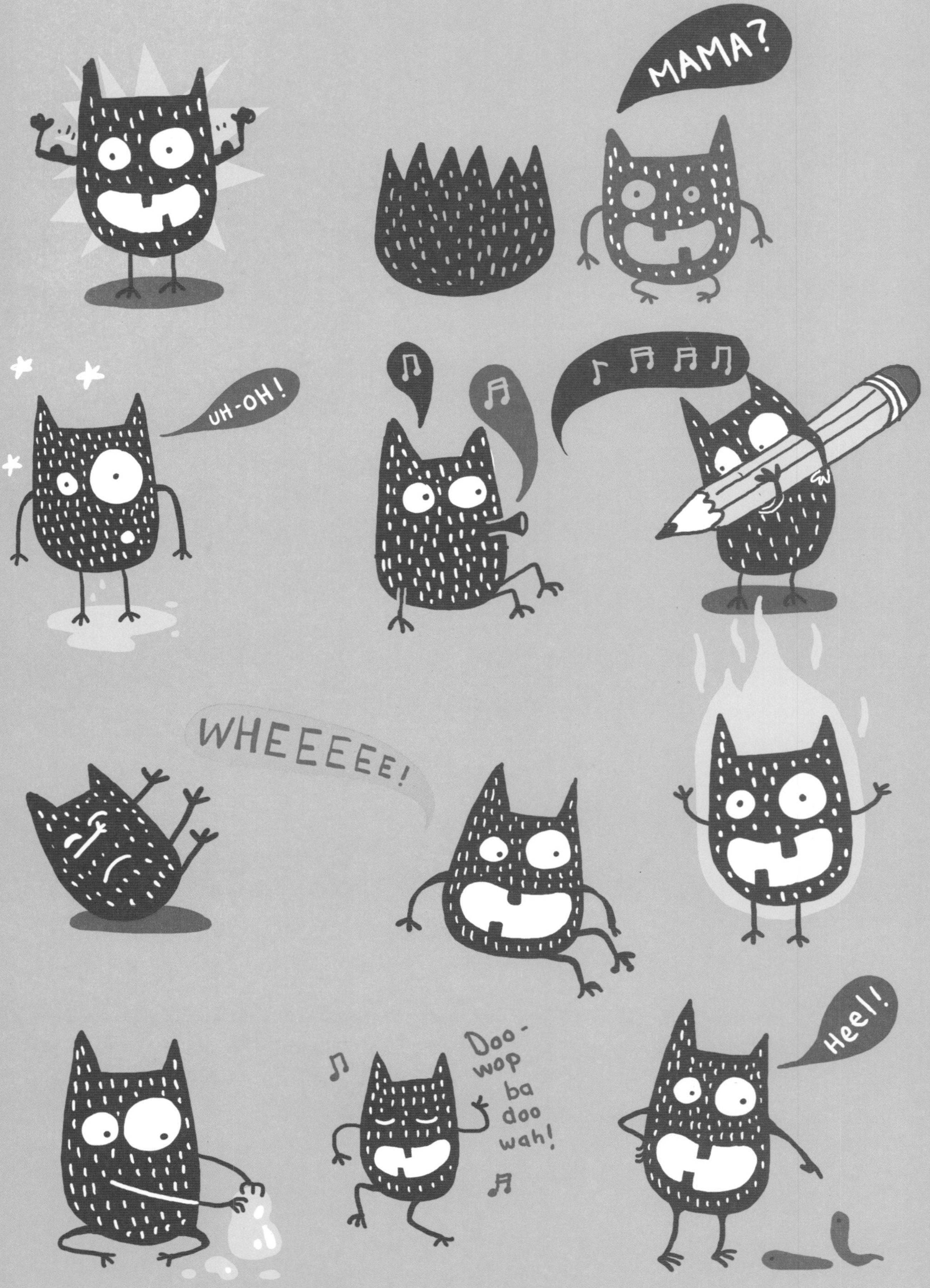
MAMA?
UH-OH!
WHEEEEEE!
Doo-
wop
ba
doo
wah!
Heel!

STORY two

A day in the office of Doctor Bugspit

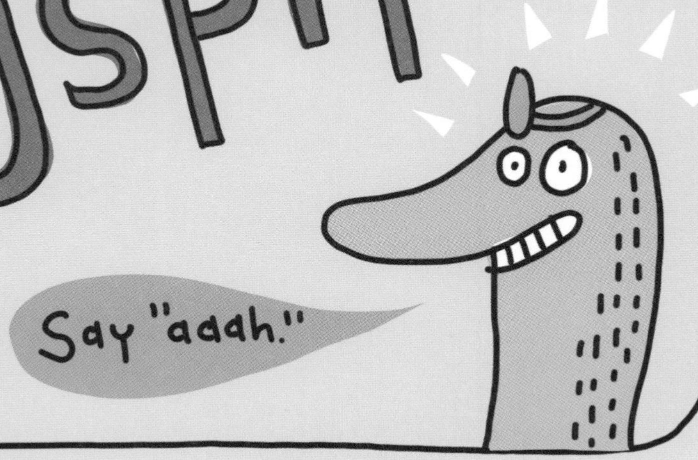

Got the cooties?

Do your ears waggle instead of wiggle?

Are you sleepwalking, skipping, and jumping?

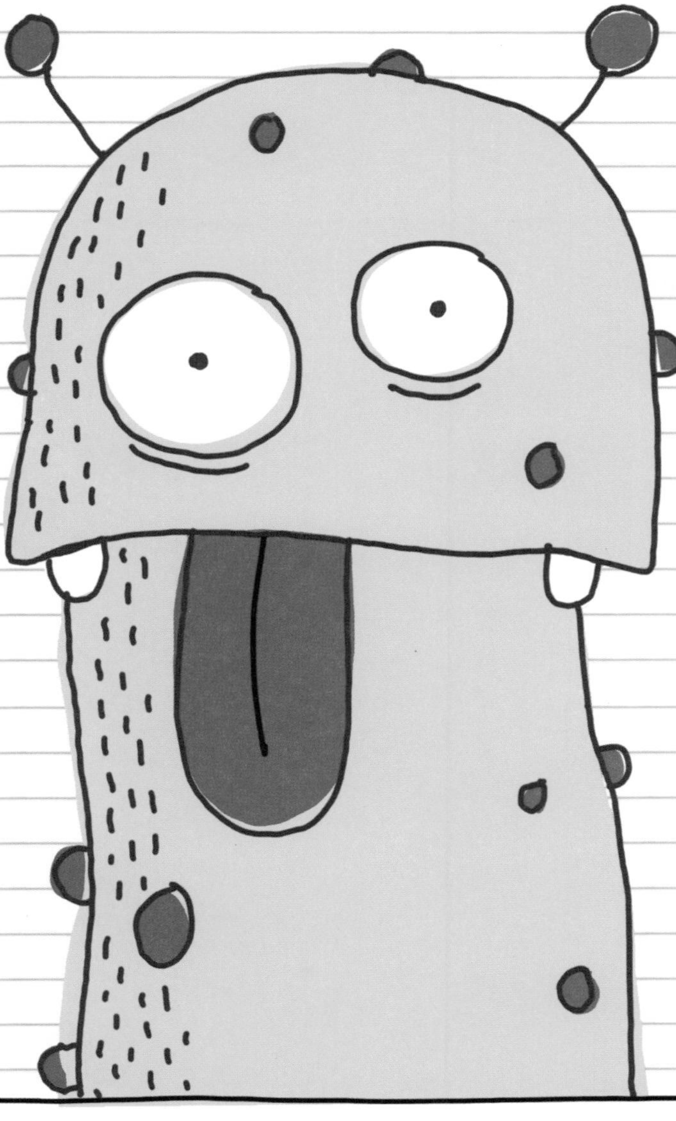

If so...

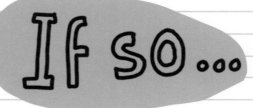

You've come to the right place.

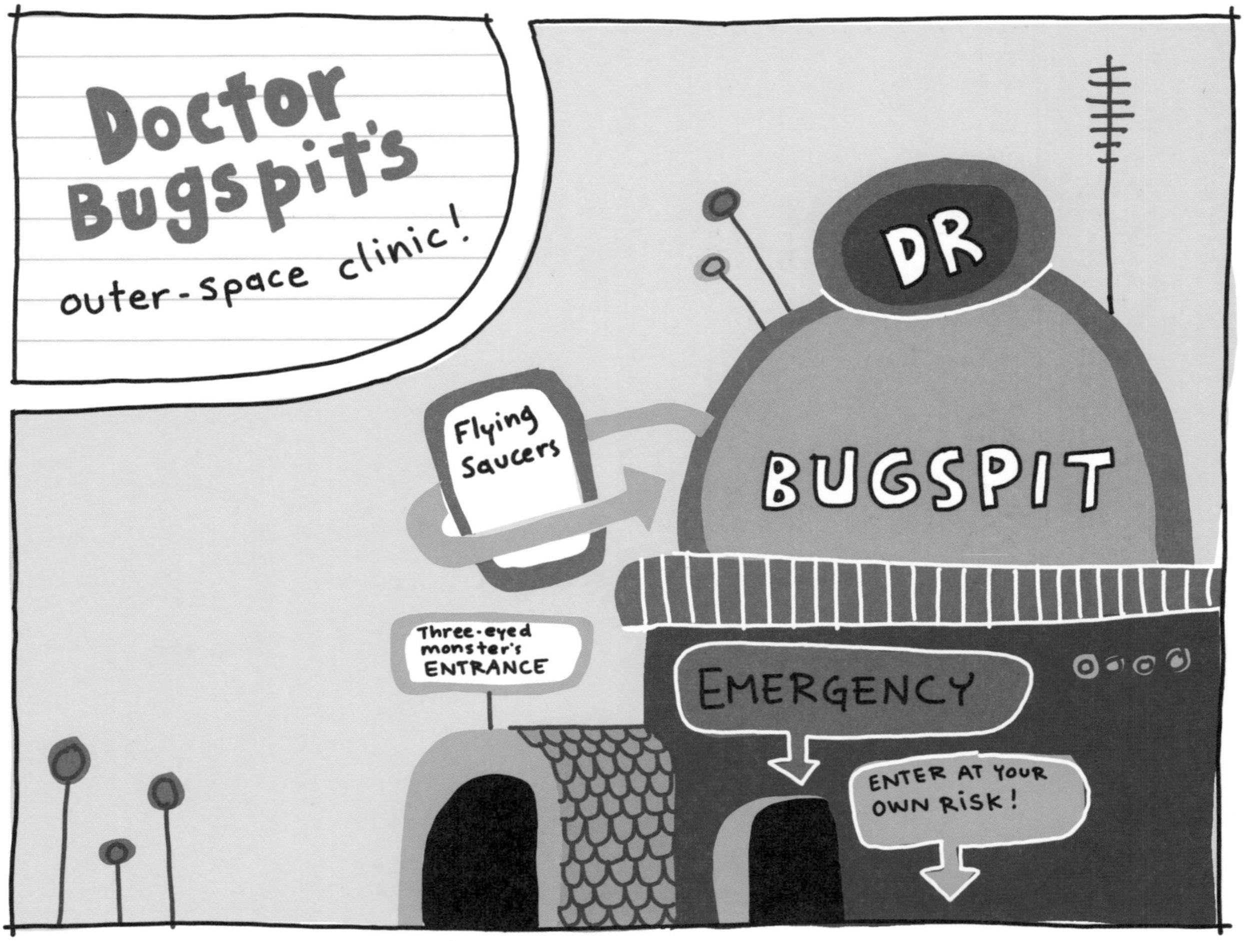
Doctor Bugspit's
outer-space clinic!
DR
BUGSPIT
Flying Saucers
Three-eyed monster's ENTRANCE
EMERGENCY
ENTER AT YOUR OWN RISK!

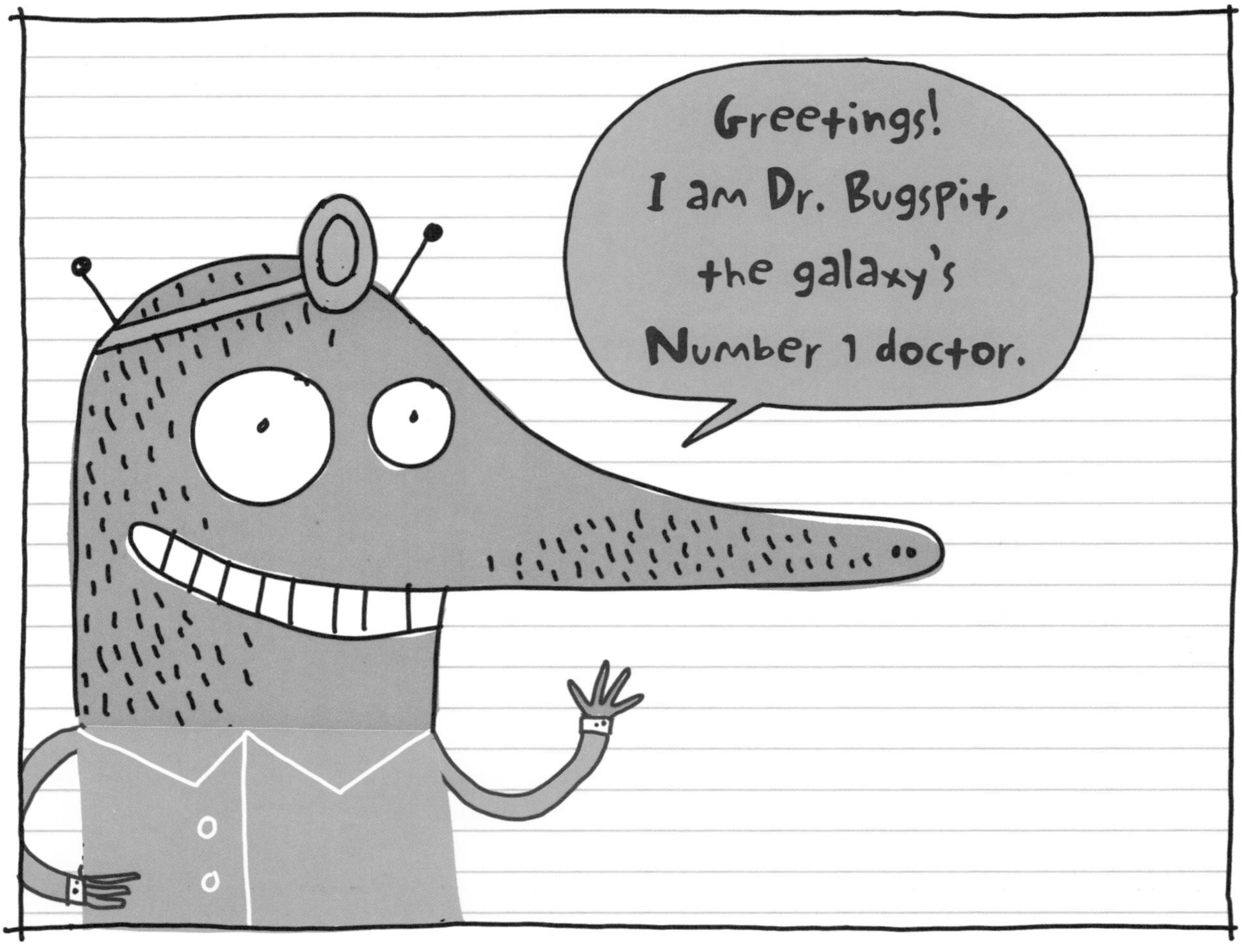
Greetings! I am Dr. Bugspit, the galaxy's Number 1 doctor.

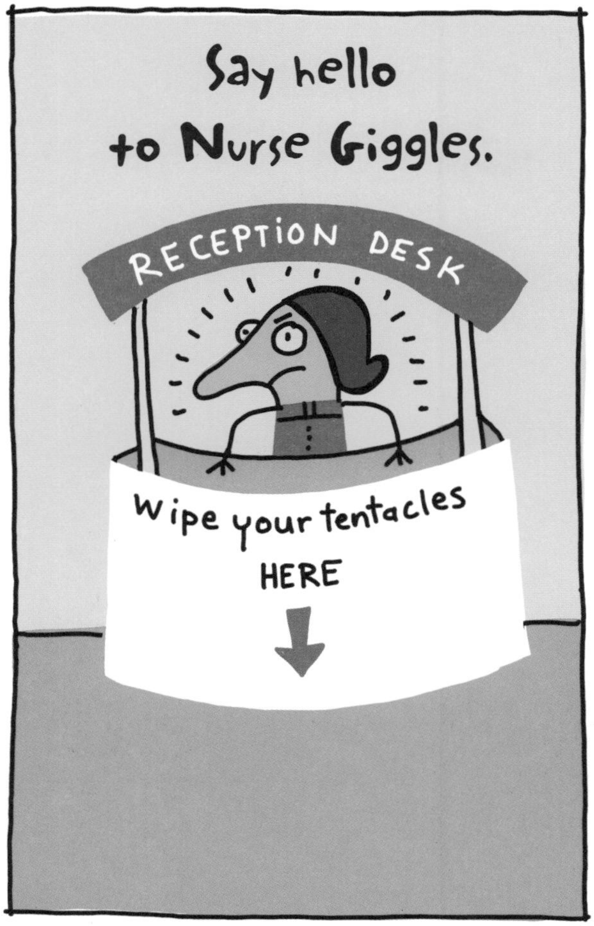
Say hello
to Nurse Giggles.
RECEPTION DESK
Wipe your tentacles
HERE

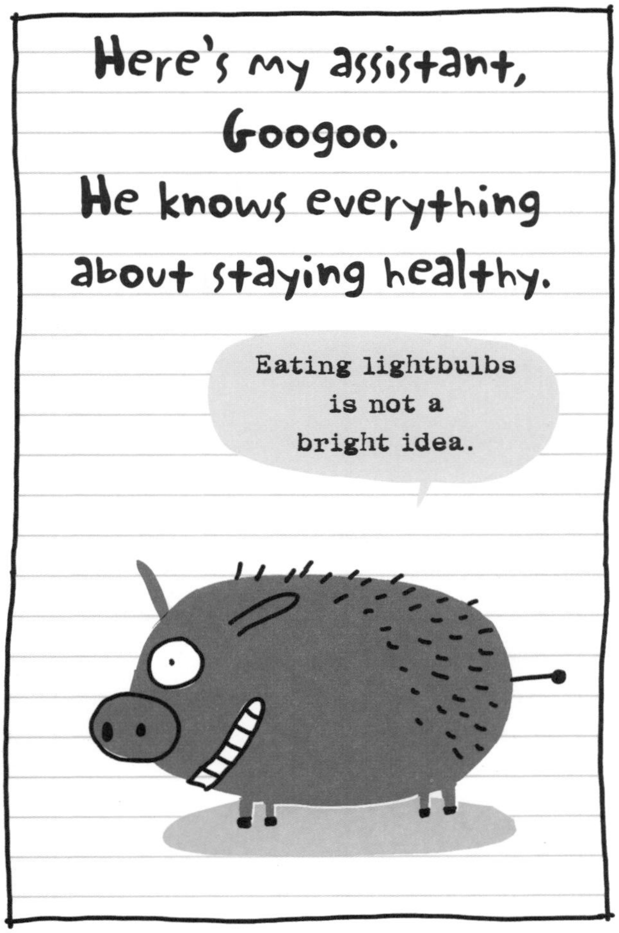
Here's my assistant,
Googoo.
He knows everything
about staying healthy.
Eating lightbulbs is not a bright idea.

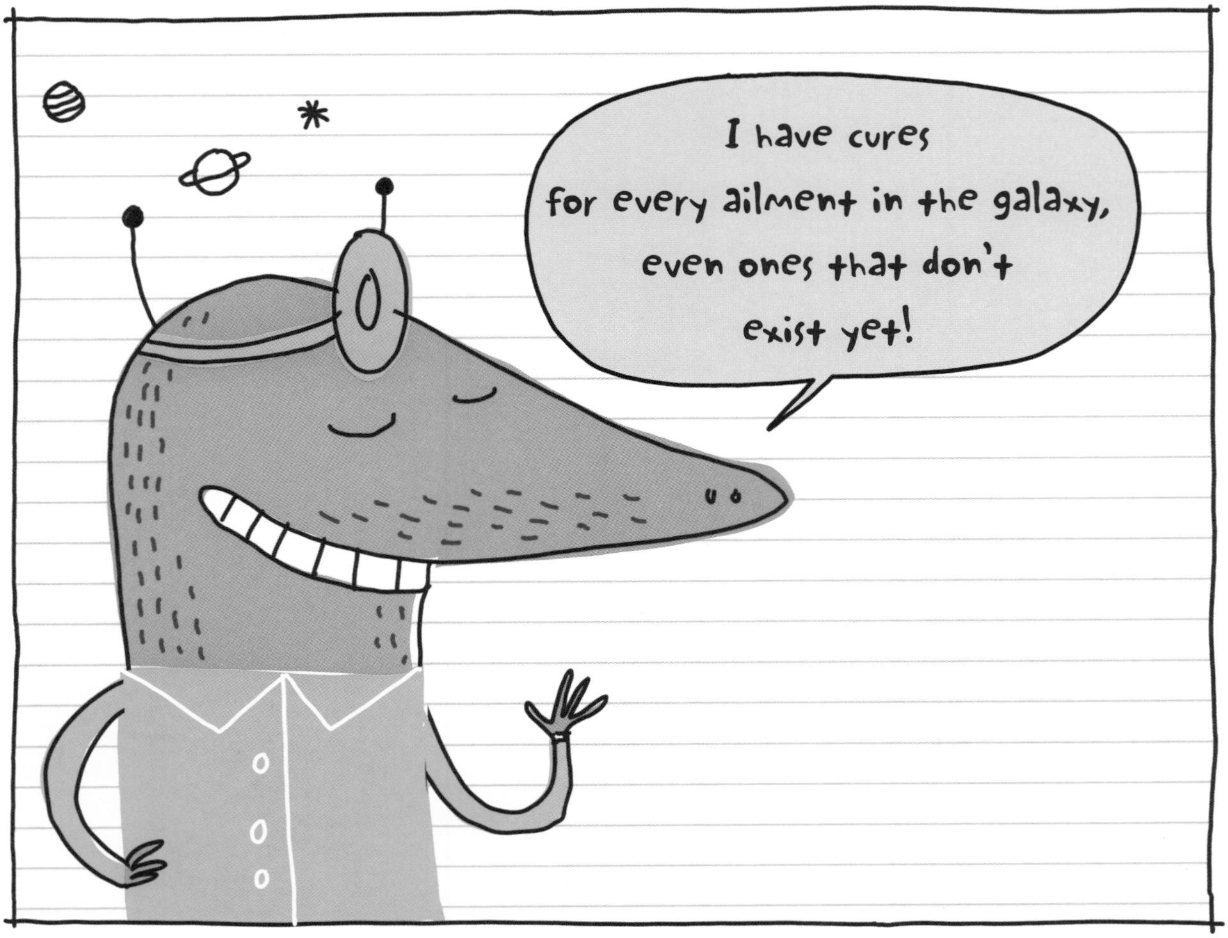
I have cures for every ailment in the galaxy, even ones that don't exist yet!

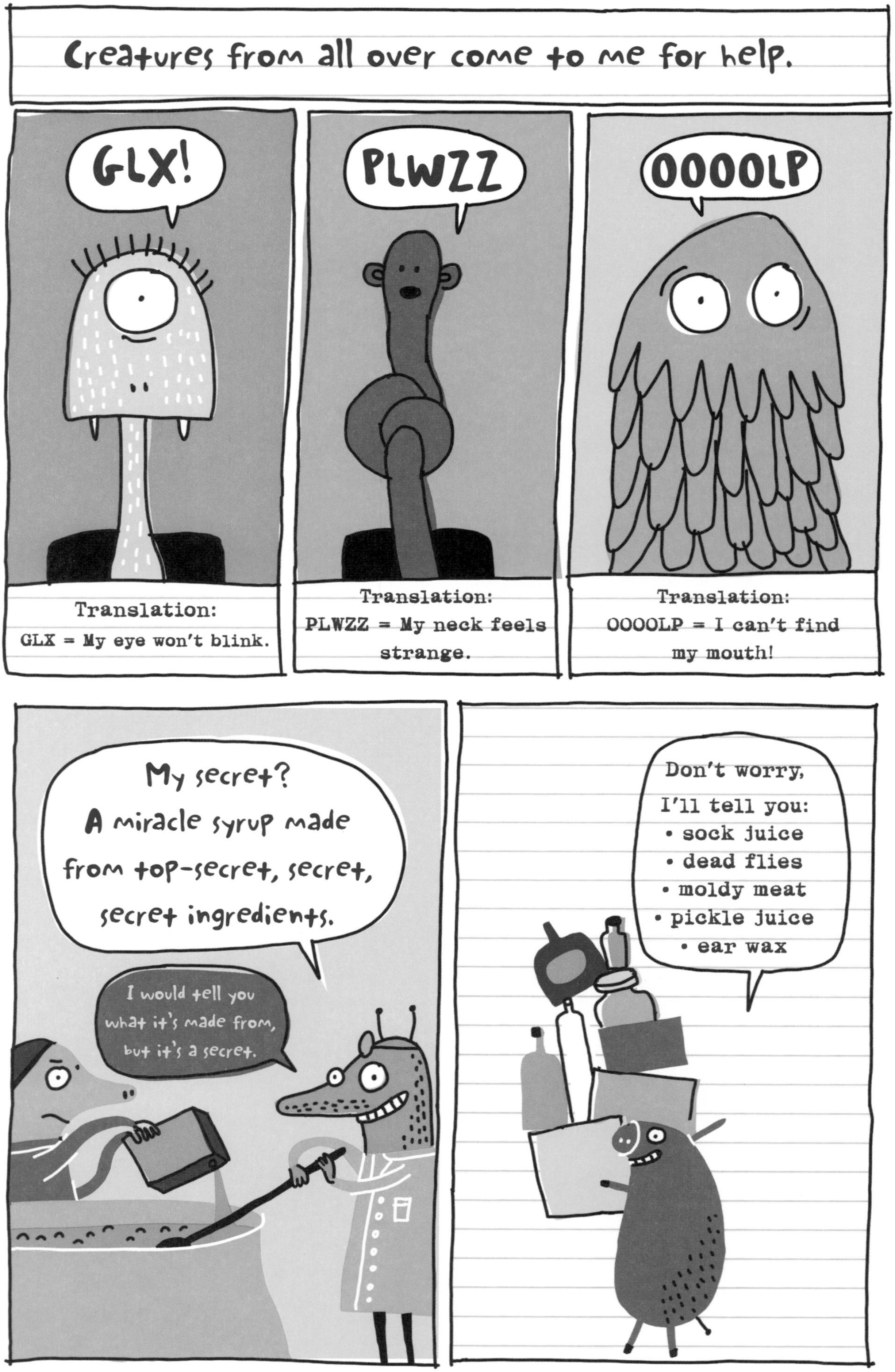
Creatures from all over come to me for help.
GLX!
Translation:
GLX = My eye won't blink.
PLWZZ
Translation:
PLWZZ = My neck feels strange.
OOOOLP
Translation:
OOOOLP = I can't find my mouth!
My secret? A miracle syrup made from top-secret, secret, secret ingredients.
I would tell you what it's made from, but it's a secret.
Don't worry, I'll tell you:
• sock juice
• dead flies
• moldy meat
• pickle juice
• ear wax

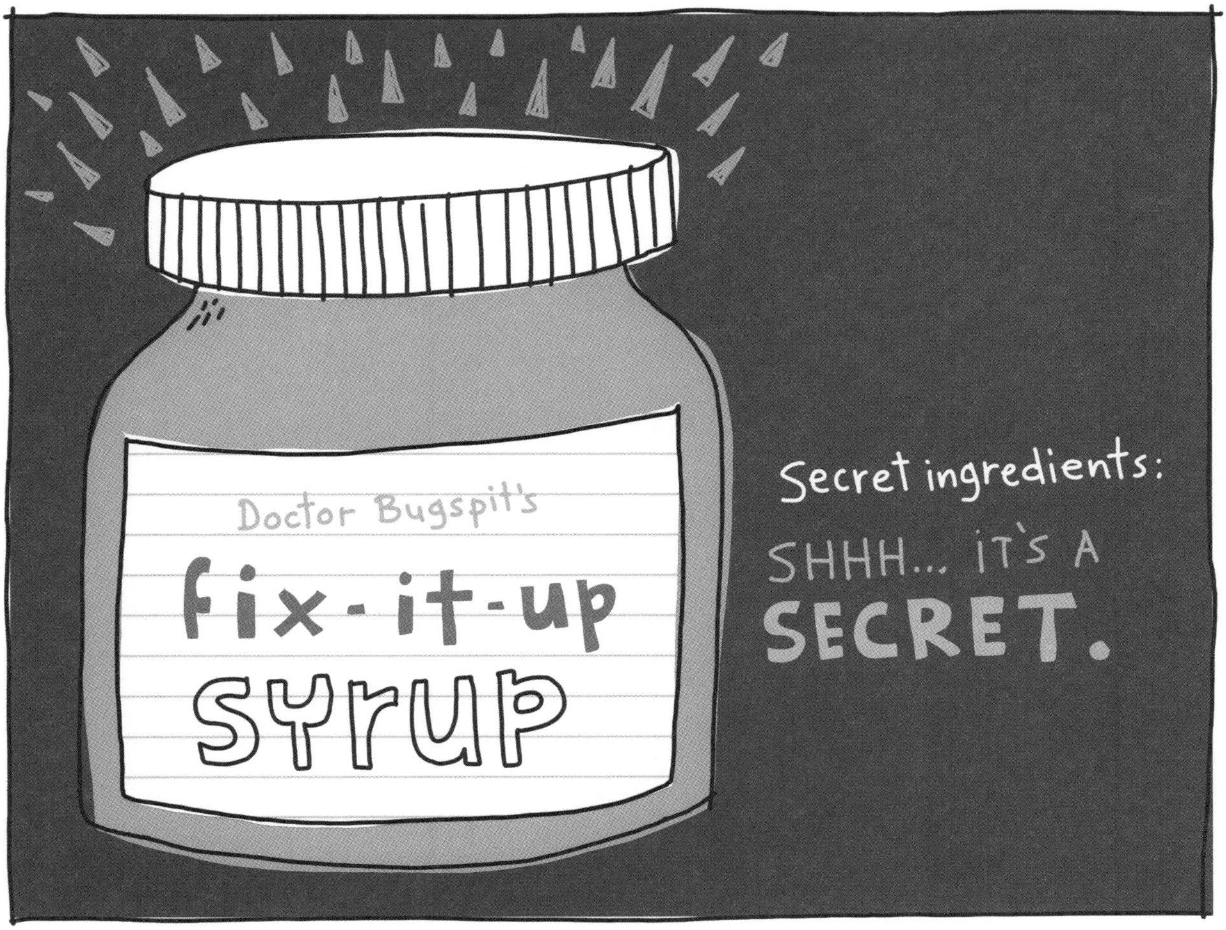
Doctor Bugspit's
fix-it-up
syrup
Secret ingredients:
SHHH... IT'S A
SECRET.

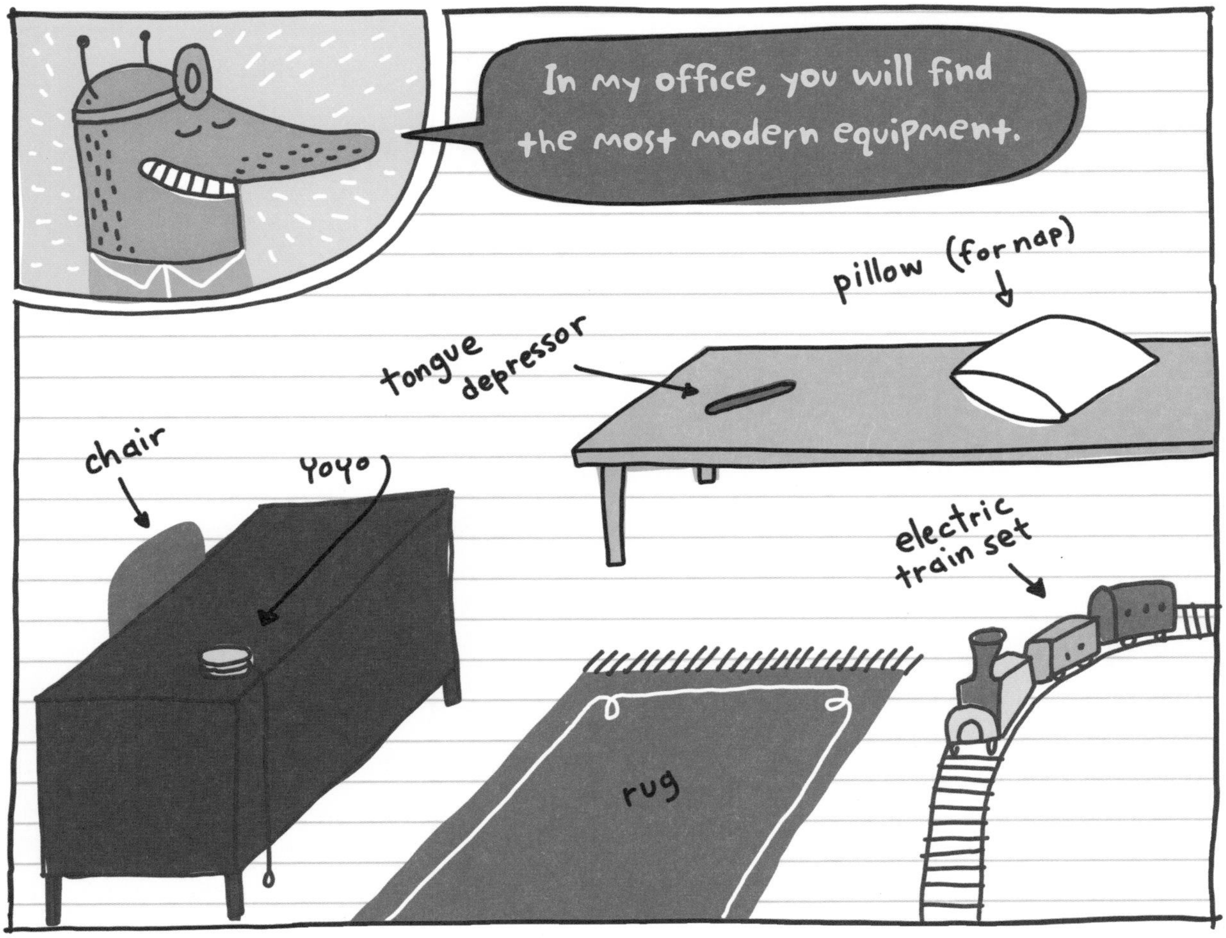
In my office, you will find the most modern equipment.
pillow (for nap)
tongue depressor
chair
yoyo
electric train set
rug

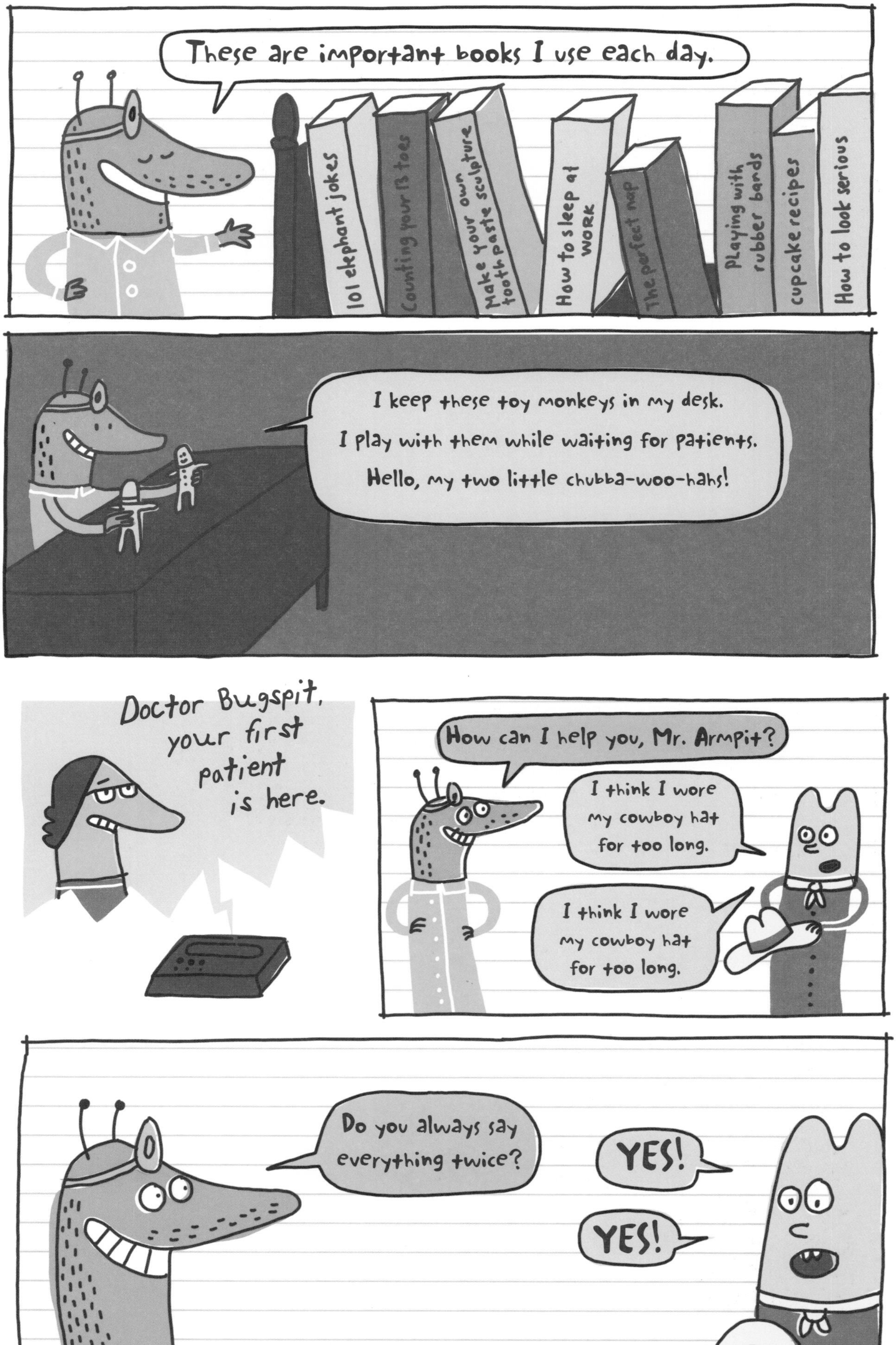
These are important books I use each day.
101 elephant jokes
Counting your 13 toes
Make your own toothpaste sculpture
How to sleep at WORK
The perfect nap
Playing with rubber bands
cupcake recipes
How to look serious
I keep these toy monkeys in my desk.
I play with them while waiting for patients.
Hello, my two little chubba-woo-hahs!
Doctor Bugspit, your first patient is here.
How can I help you, Mr. Armpit?
I think I wore my cowboy hat for too long.
I think I wore my cowboy hat for too long.
Do you always say everything twice?
YES!
YES!

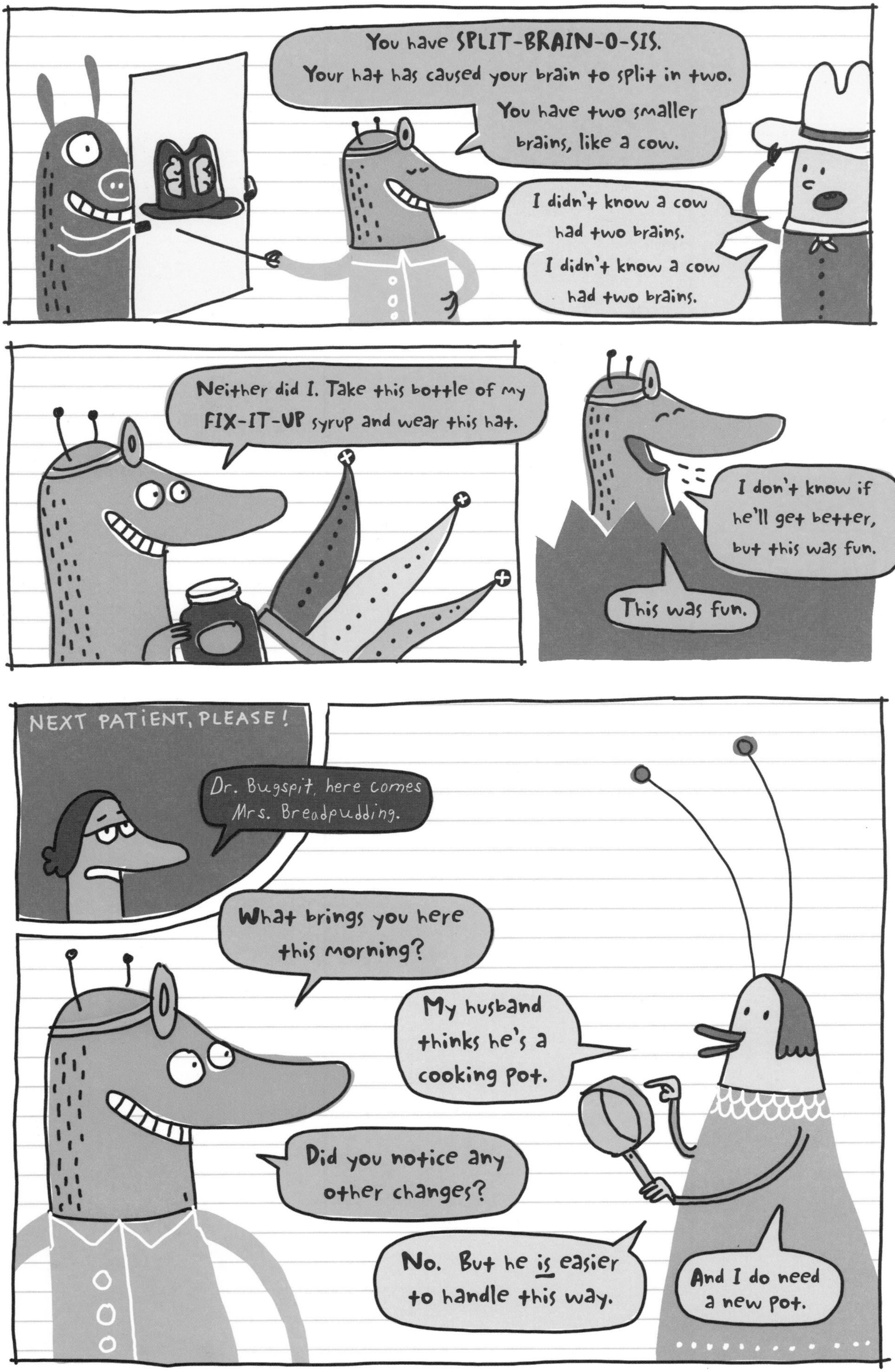

You have SPLIT-BRAIN-O-SIS. Your hat has caused your brain to split in two.
You have two smaller brains, like a cow.
I didn't know a cow had two brains.
I didn't know a cow had two brains.
Neither did I. Take this bottle of my FIX-IT-UP syrup and wear this hat.
I don't know if he'll get better, but this was fun.
This was fun.
NEXT PATIENT, PLEASE!
Dr. Bugspit, here comes Mrs. Breadpudding.
What brings you here this morning?
My husband thinks he's a cooking pot.
Did you notice any other changes?
No. But he is easier to handle this way.
And I do need a new pot.

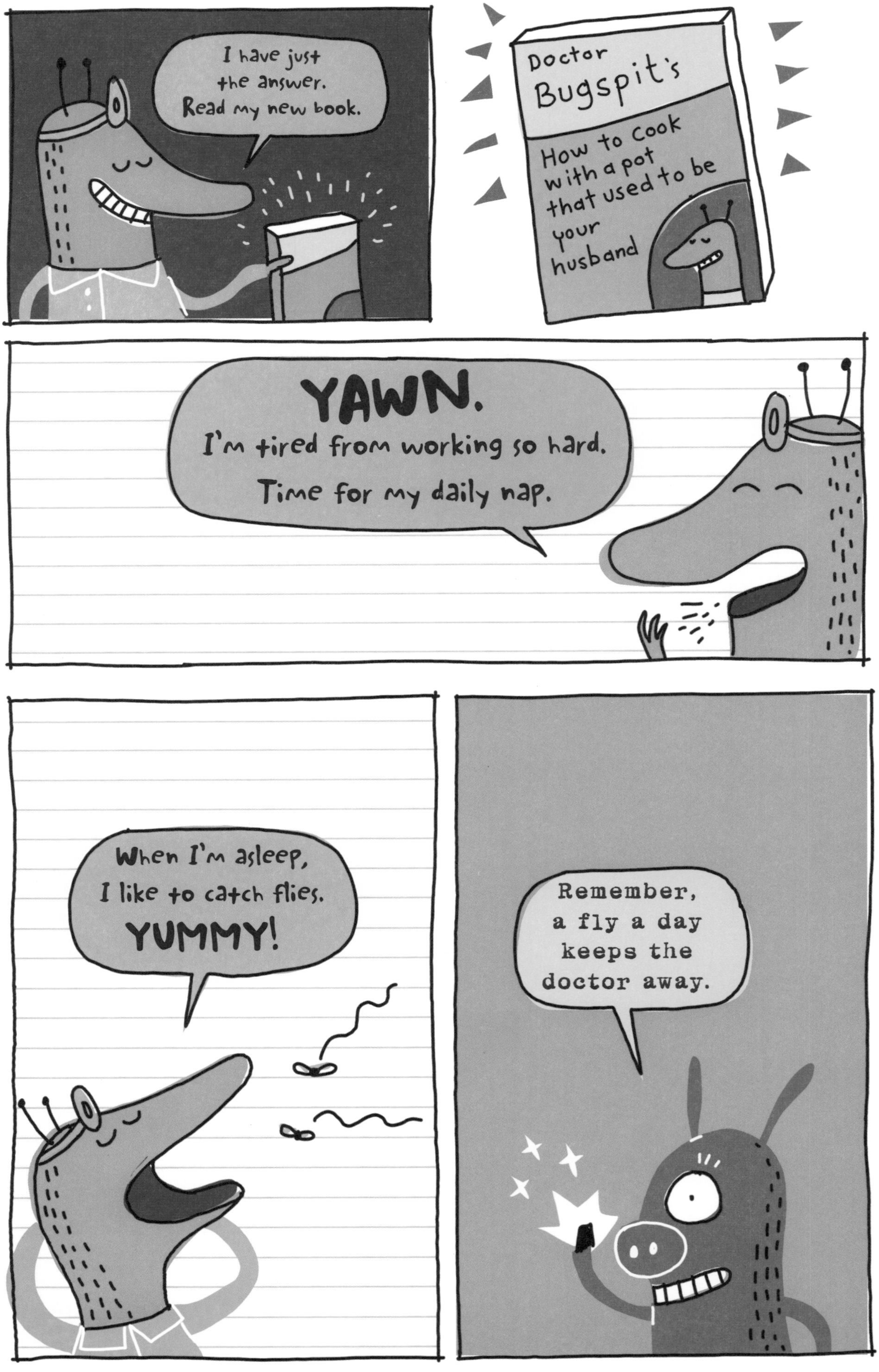
I have just the answer. Read my new book.
Doctor Bugspit's
How to cook with a pot that used to be your husband
YAWN. I'm tired from working so hard. Time for my daily nap.
When I'm asleep, I like to catch flies. YUMMY!
Remember, a fly a day keeps the doctor away.

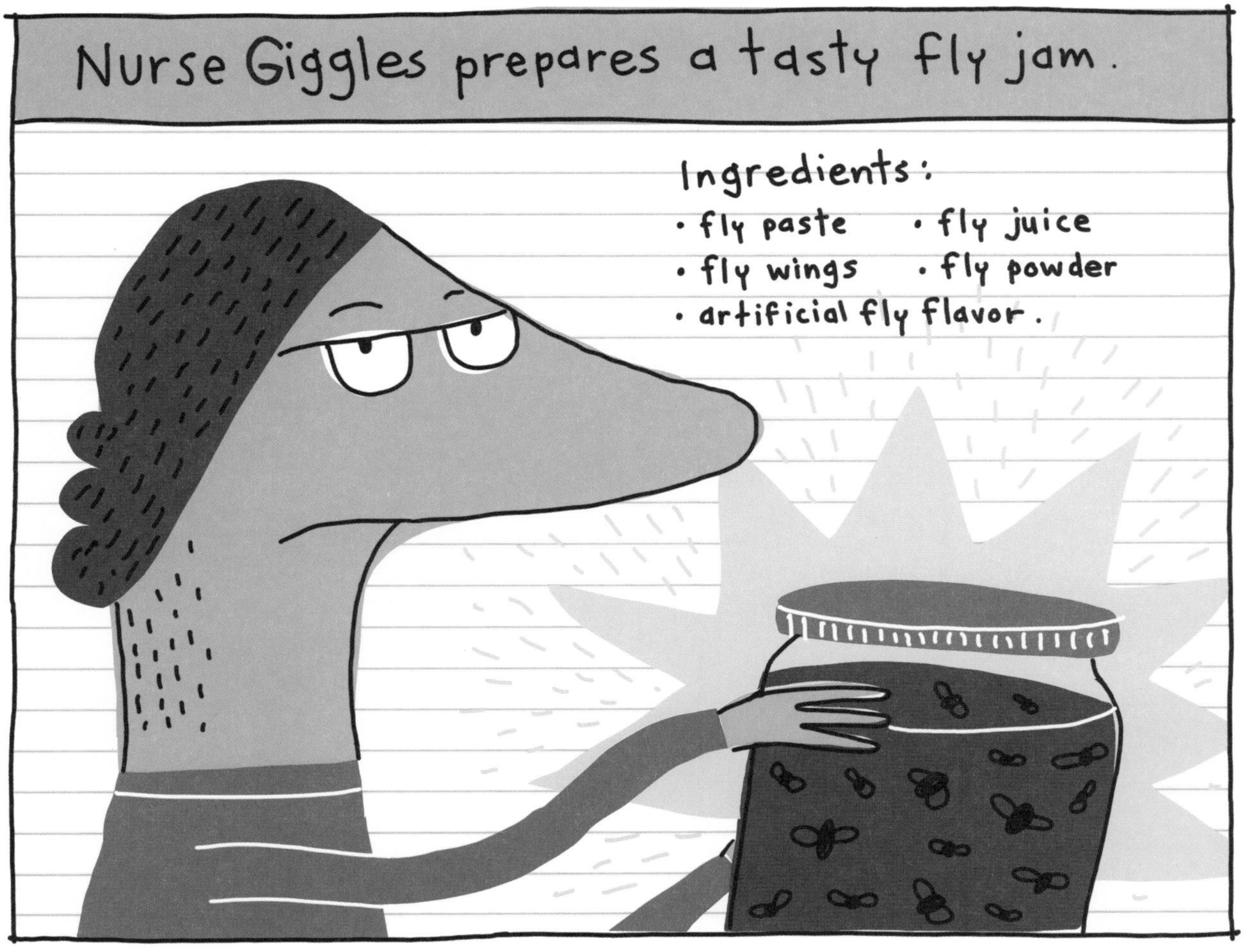
Nurse Giggles prepares a tasty fly jam.
Ingredients:
• fly paste
• fly juice
• fly wings
• fly powder
• artificial fly flavor.

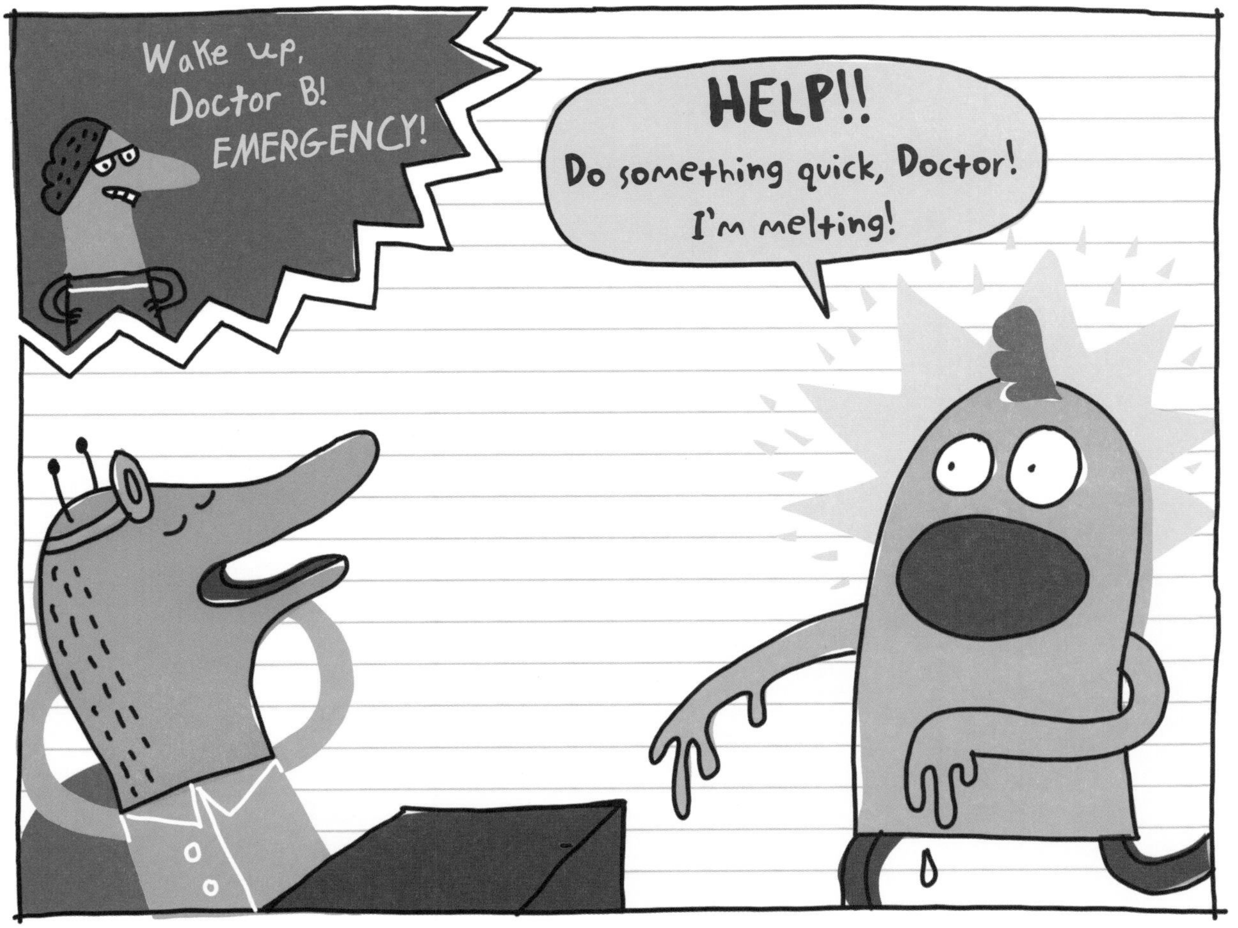
Wake up, Doctor B! EMERGENCY!
HELP!!
Do something quick, Doctor! I'm melting!

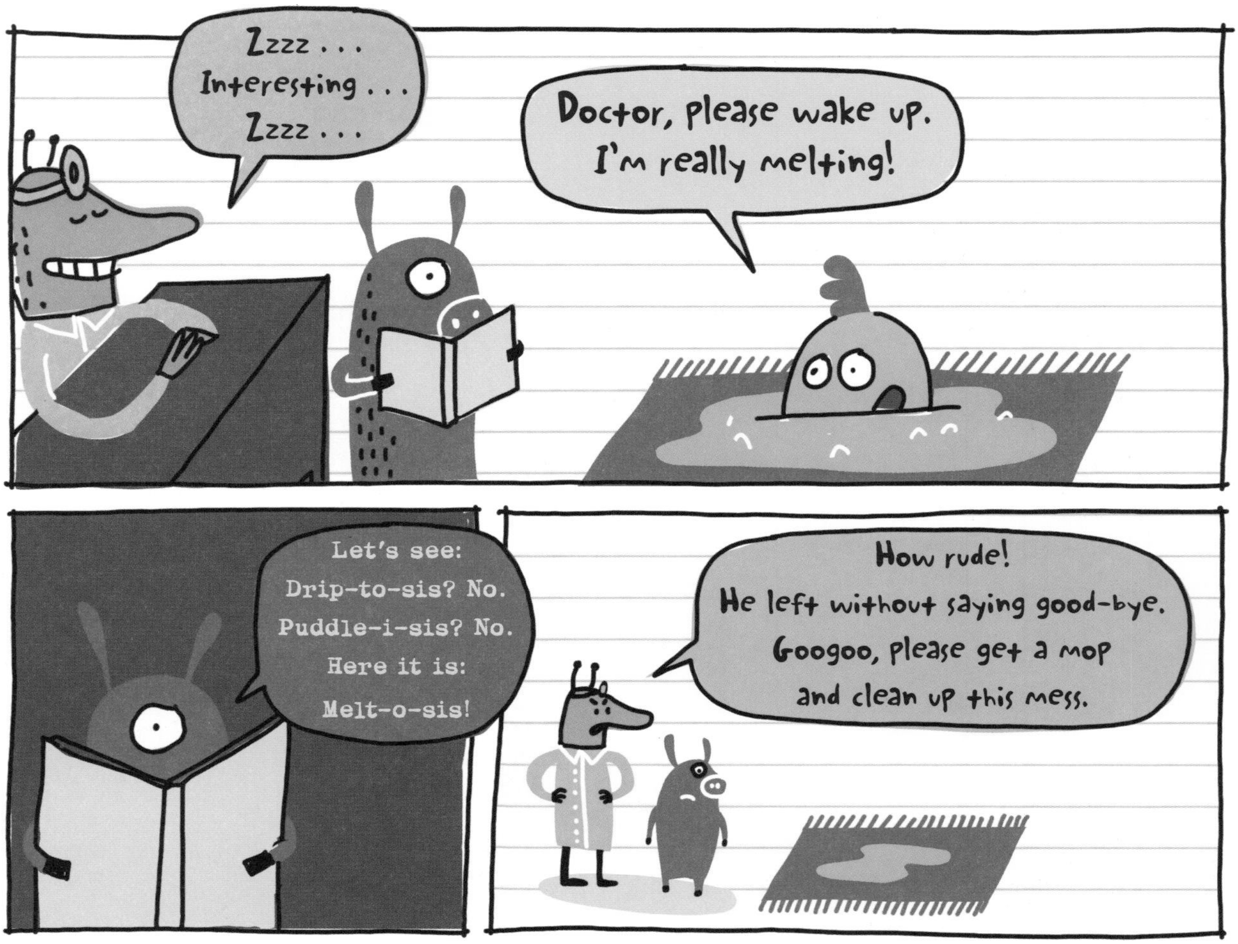
Zzzz . . .
Interesting . . .
Zzzz . . .
Doctor, please wake up.
I'm really melting!
Let's see:
Drip-to-sis? No.
Puddle-i-sis? No.
Here it is:
Melt-o-sis!
How rude!
He left without saying good-bye.
Googoo, please get a mop
and clean up this mess.

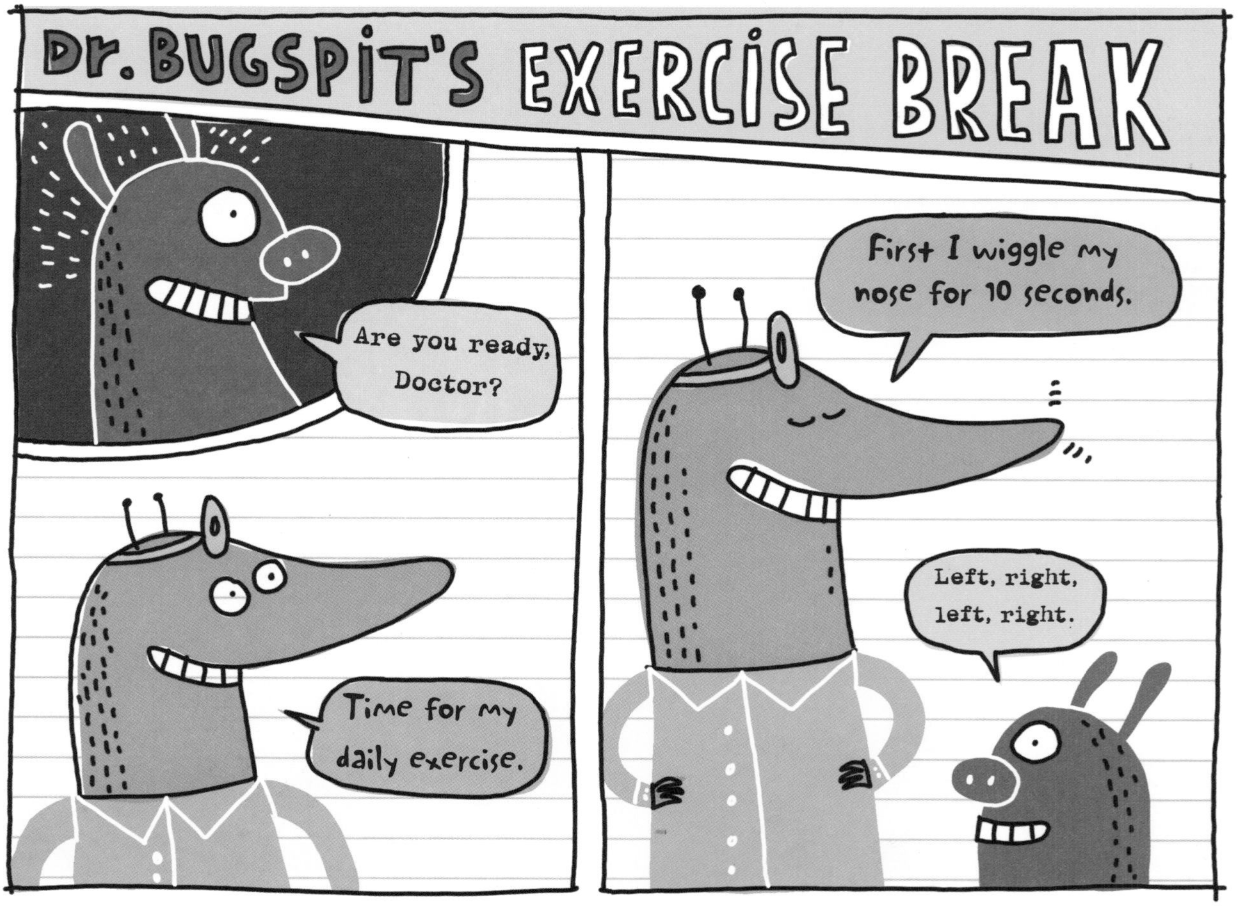
Dr. BUGSPIT'S EXERCISE BREAK
Are you ready, Doctor?
Time for my daily exercise.
First I wiggle my nose for 10 seconds.
Left, right, left, right.

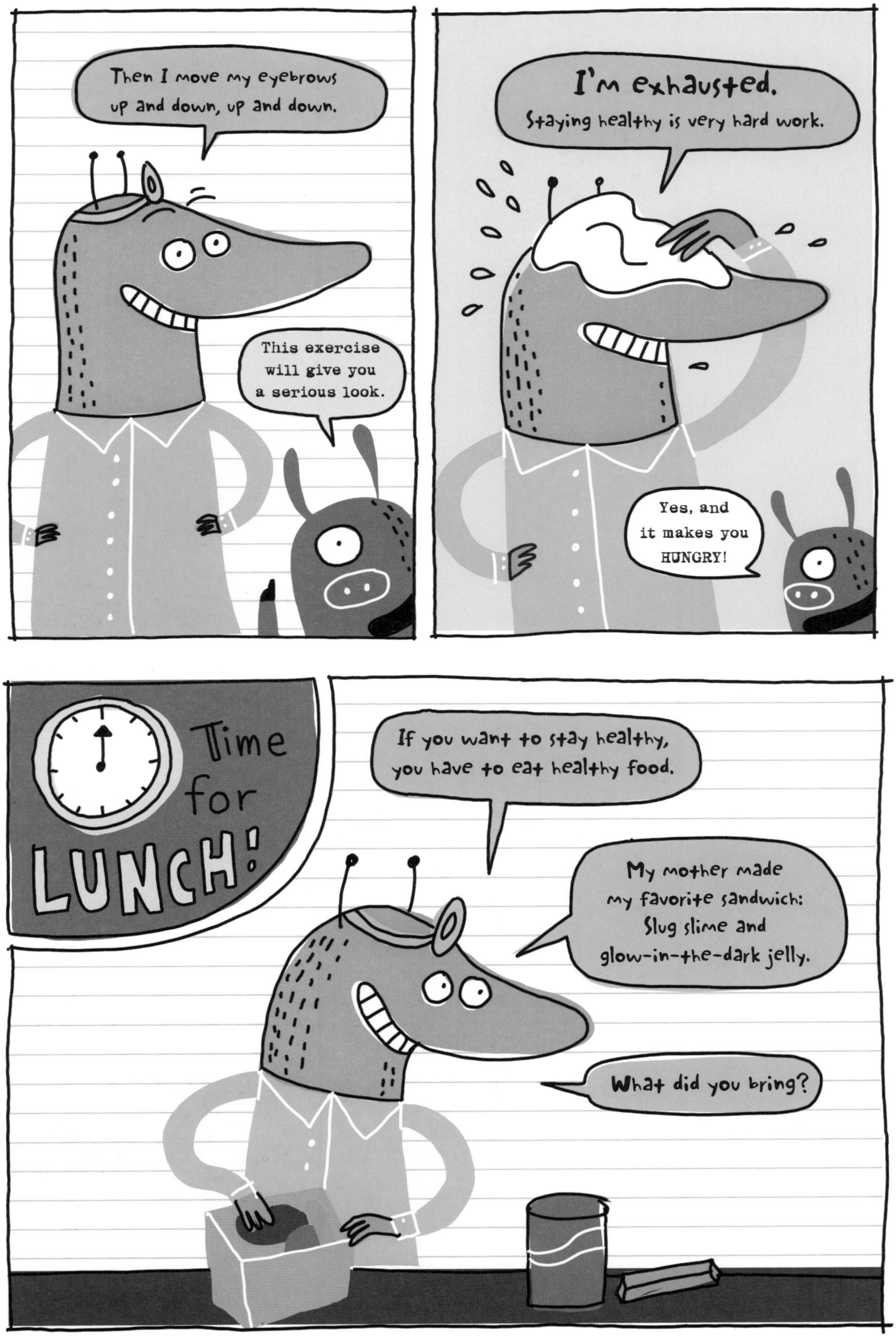

Then I move my eyebrows up and down, up and down.
This exercise will give you a serious look.
I'm exhausted.
Staying healthy is very hard work.
Yes, and it makes you HUNGRY!
Time for LUNCH!
If you want to stay healthy, you have to eat healthy food.
My mother made my favorite sandwich: Slug slime and glow-in-the-dark jelly.
What did you bring?

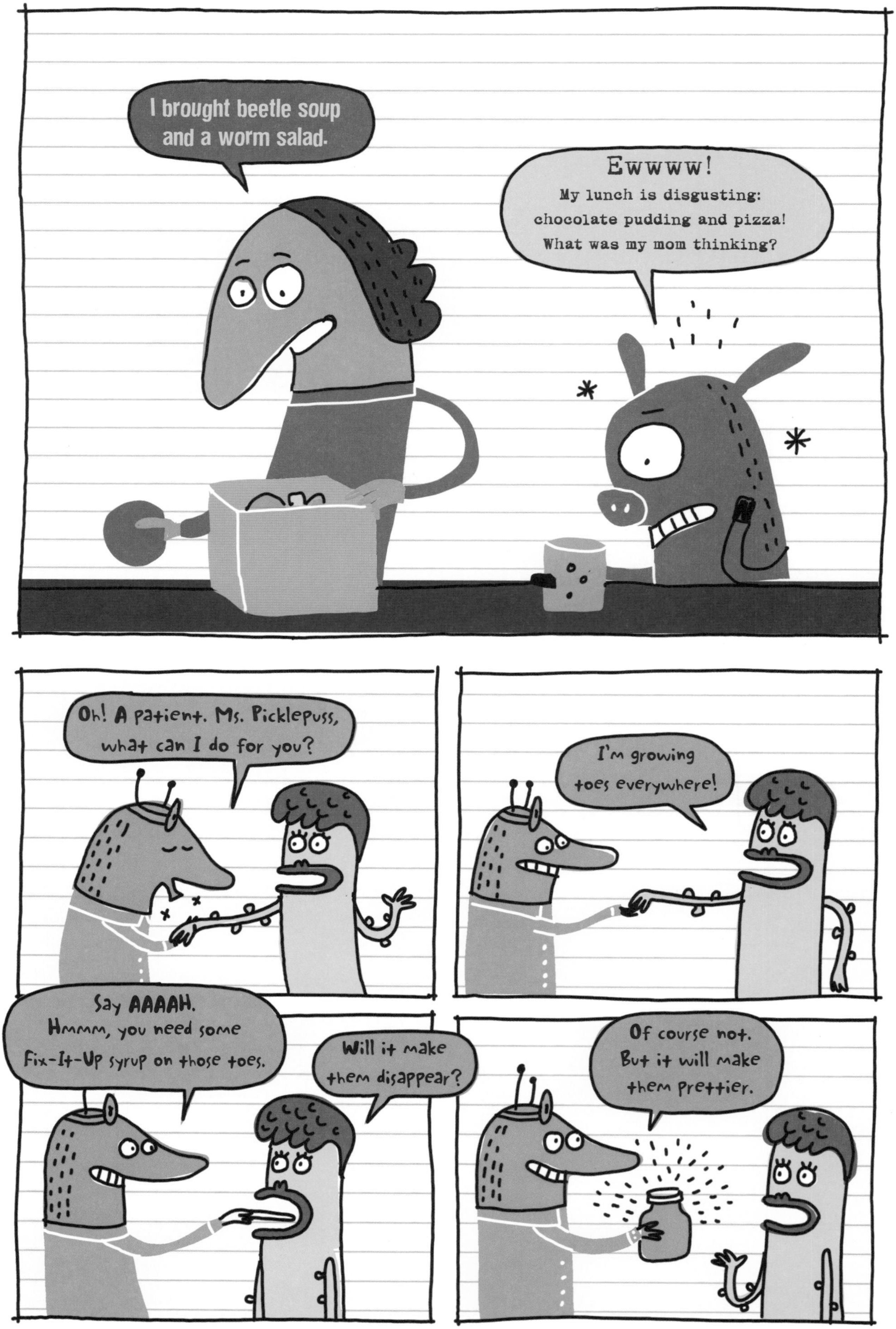

I brought beetle soup and a worm salad.
Ewwww! My lunch is disgusting: chocolate pudding and pizza! What was my mom thinking?
Oh! A patient. Ms. Picklepuss, what can I do for you?
I'm growing toes everywhere!
Say AAAAH. Hmmm, you need some Fix-It-Up syrup on those toes.
Will it make them disappear?
Of course not. But it will make them prettier.

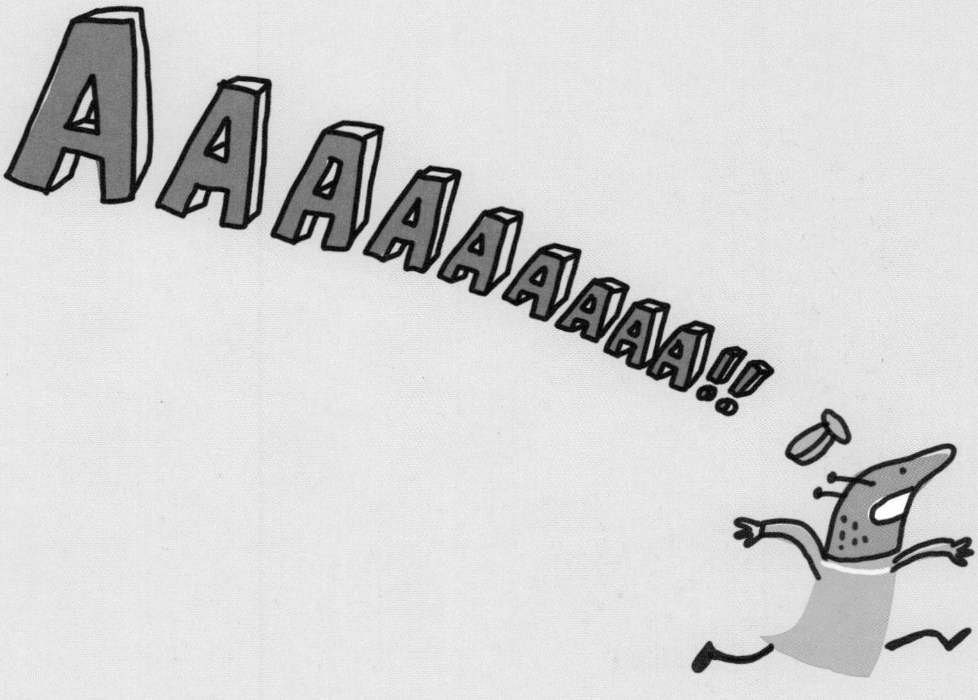
AAAAAAAAA!!

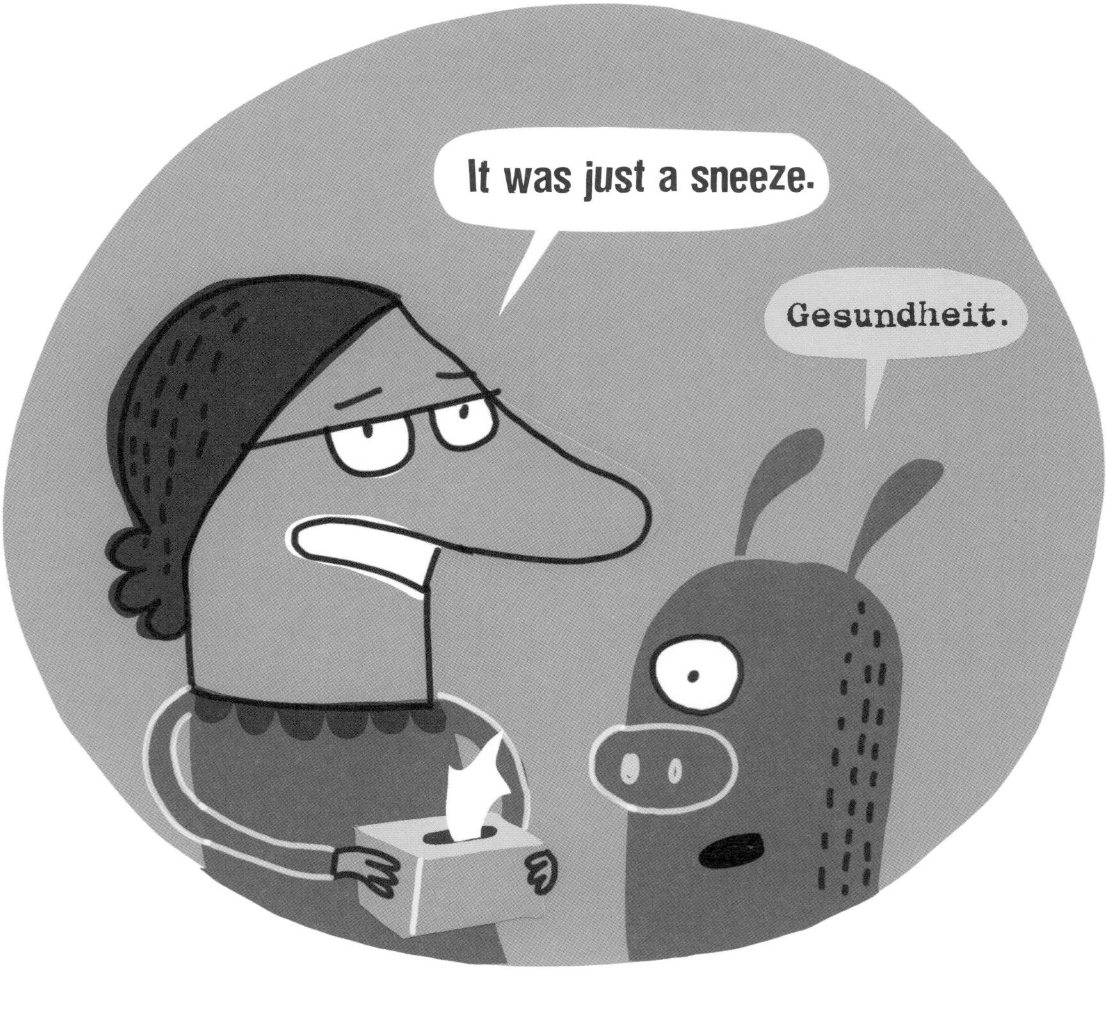
It was just a sneeze.
Gesundheit.

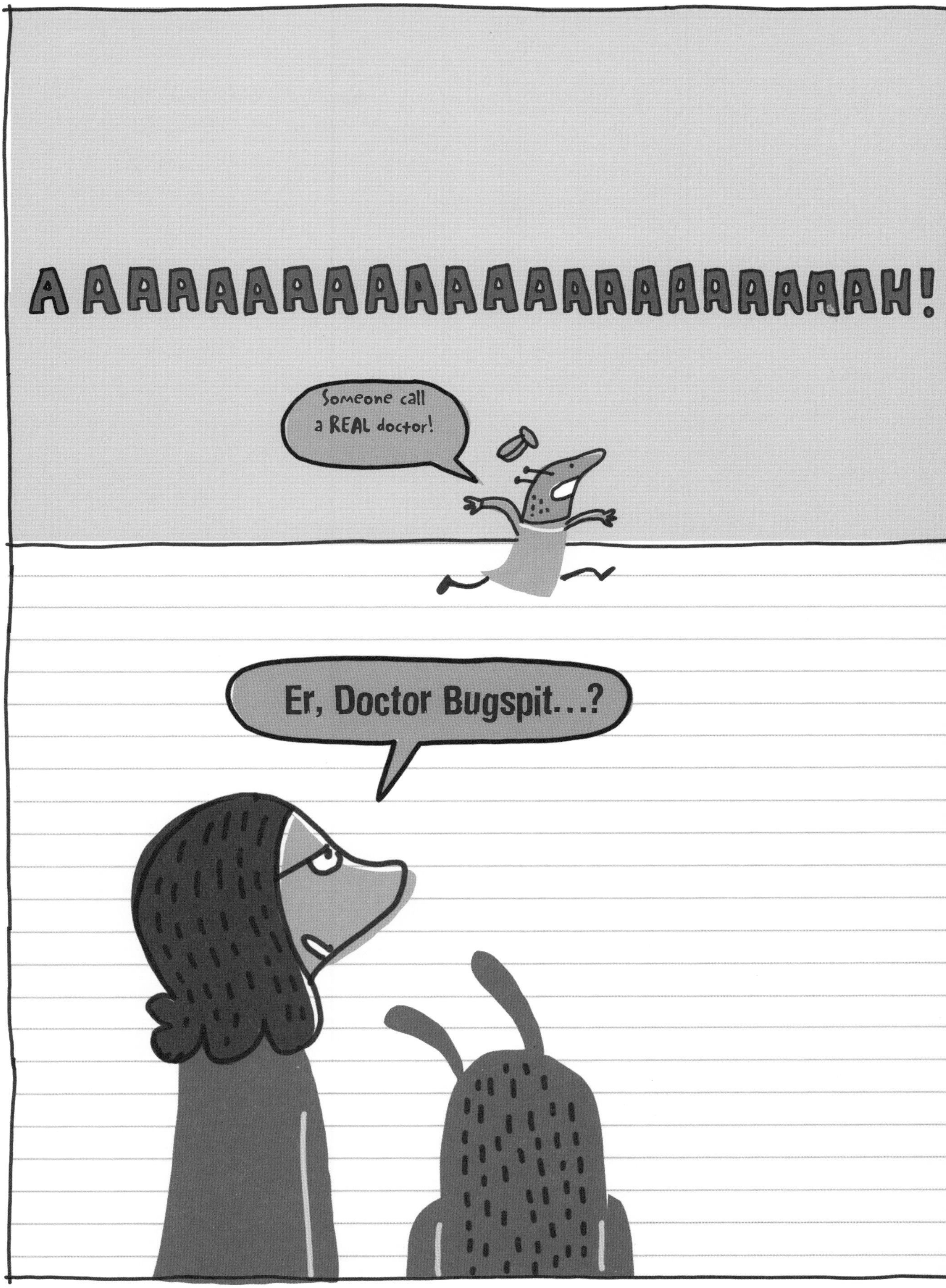
AAAAAAAAAAAAAAAAAAAAAAAH!
Someone call a REAL doctor!
Er, Doctor Bugspit...?

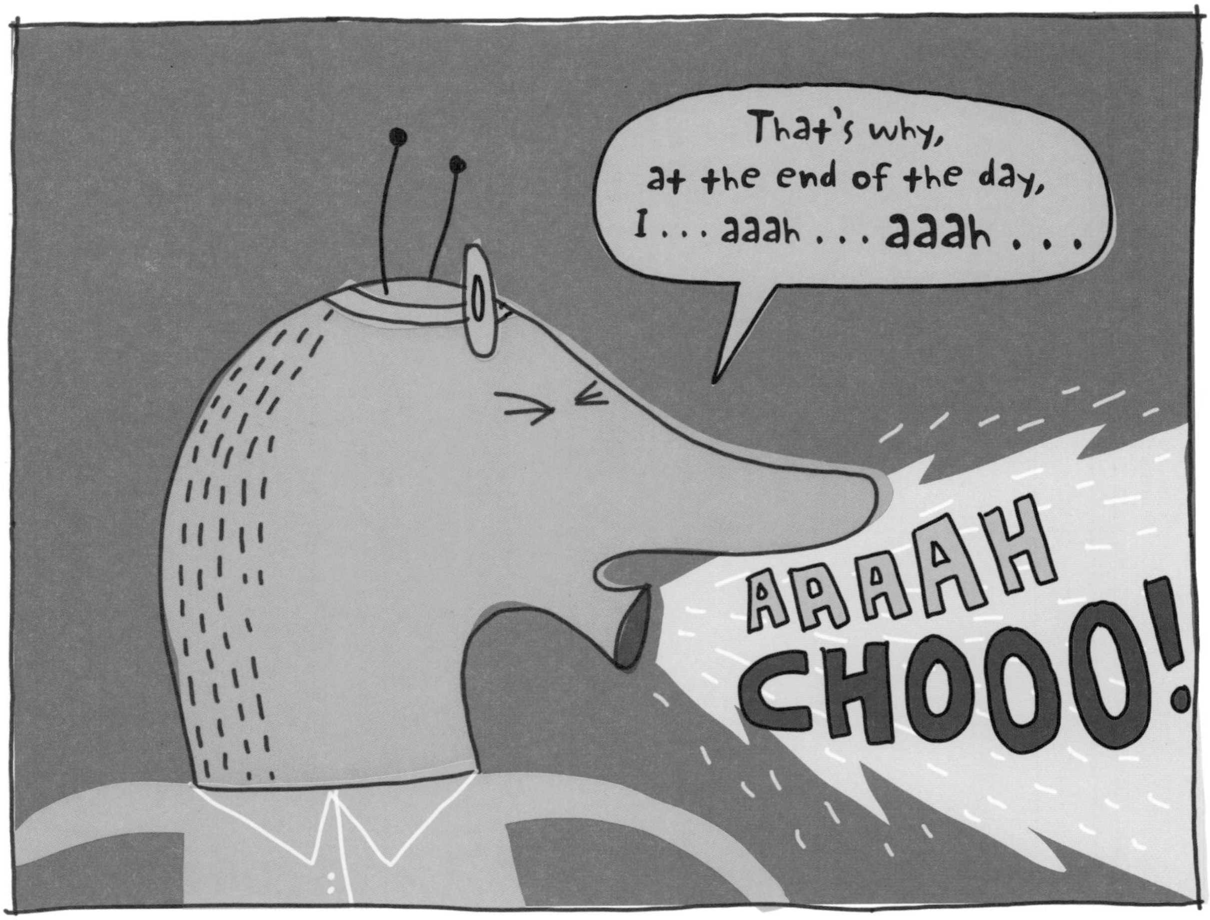
That's why,
at the end of the day,
I . . . aaah . . . aaah . . .
AAAAH
CHOOO!

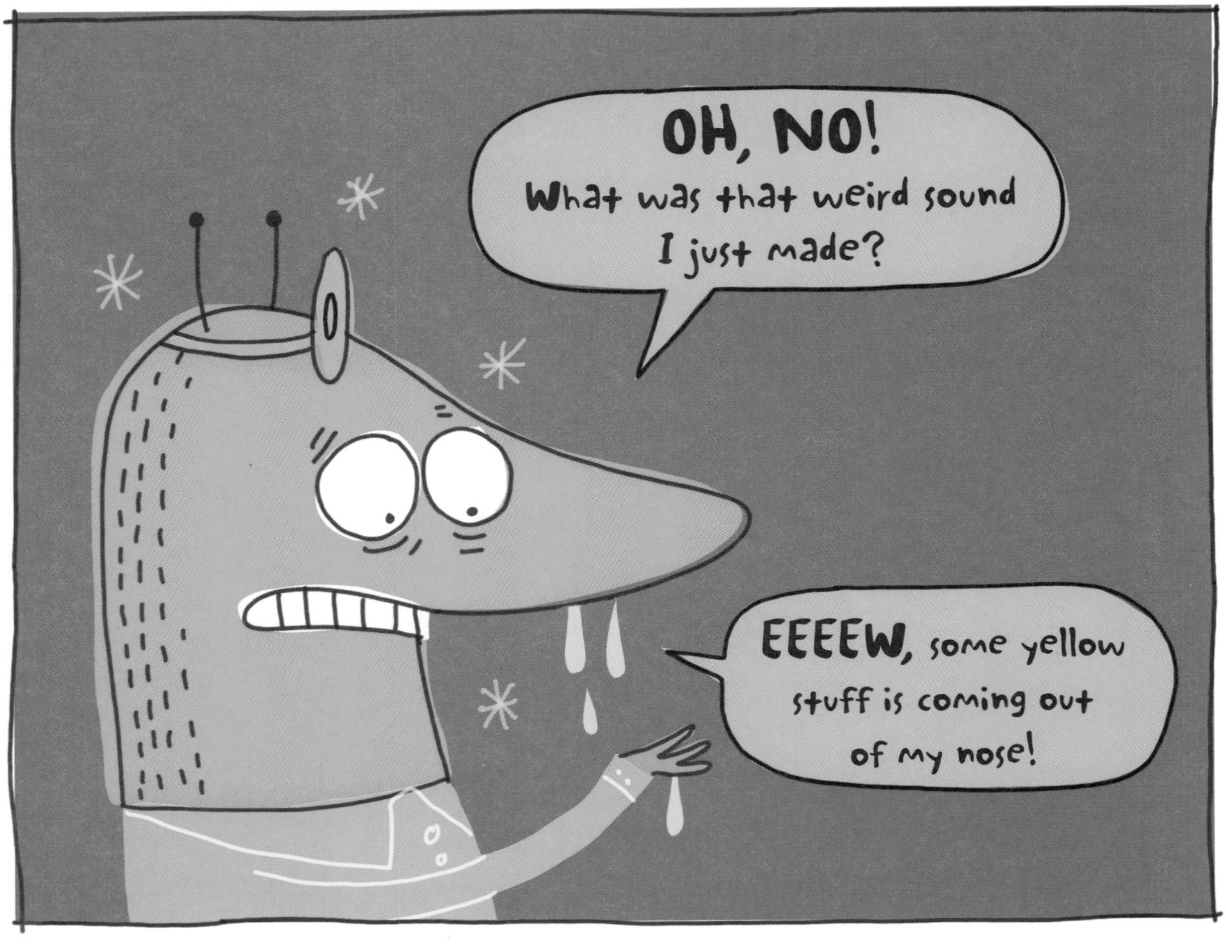
OH, NO!
What was that weird sound
I just made?
EEEEW, some yellow
stuff is coming out
of my nose!

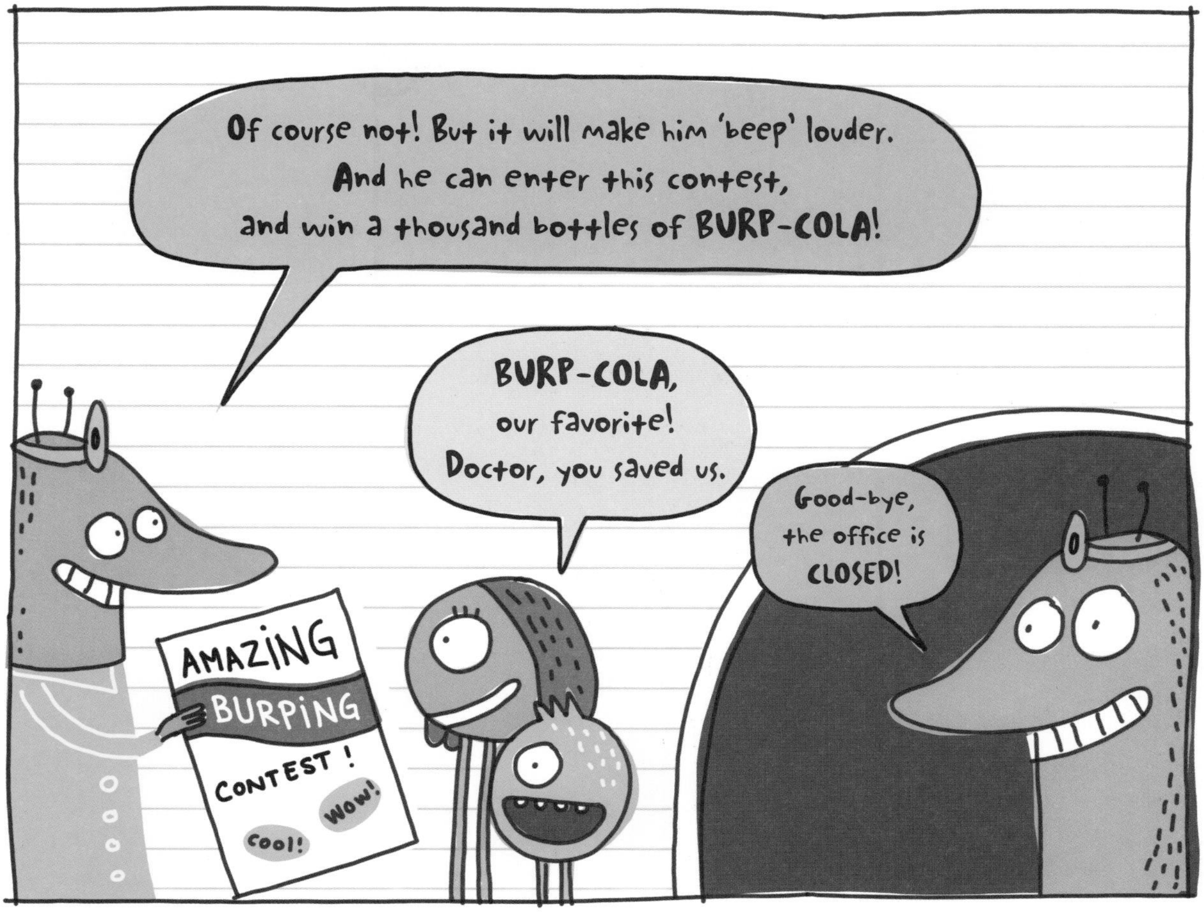
Of course not! But it will make him 'beep' louder. And he can enter this contest, and win a thousand bottles of BURP-COLA!
AMAZING BURPING CONTEST! COOL! WOW!
BURP-COLA, our favorite! Doctor, you saved us.
Good-bye, the office is CLOSED!

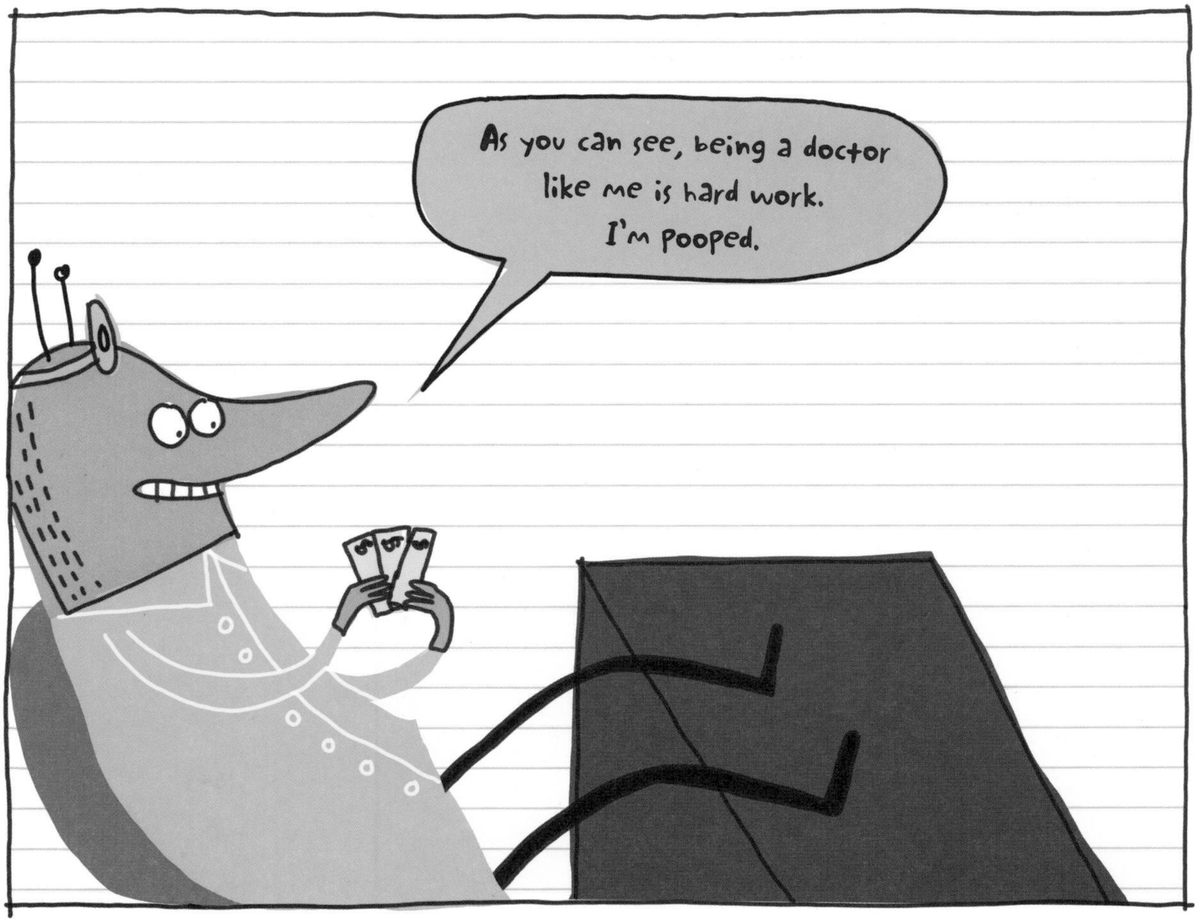
As you can see, being a doctor like me is hard work. I'm pooped.

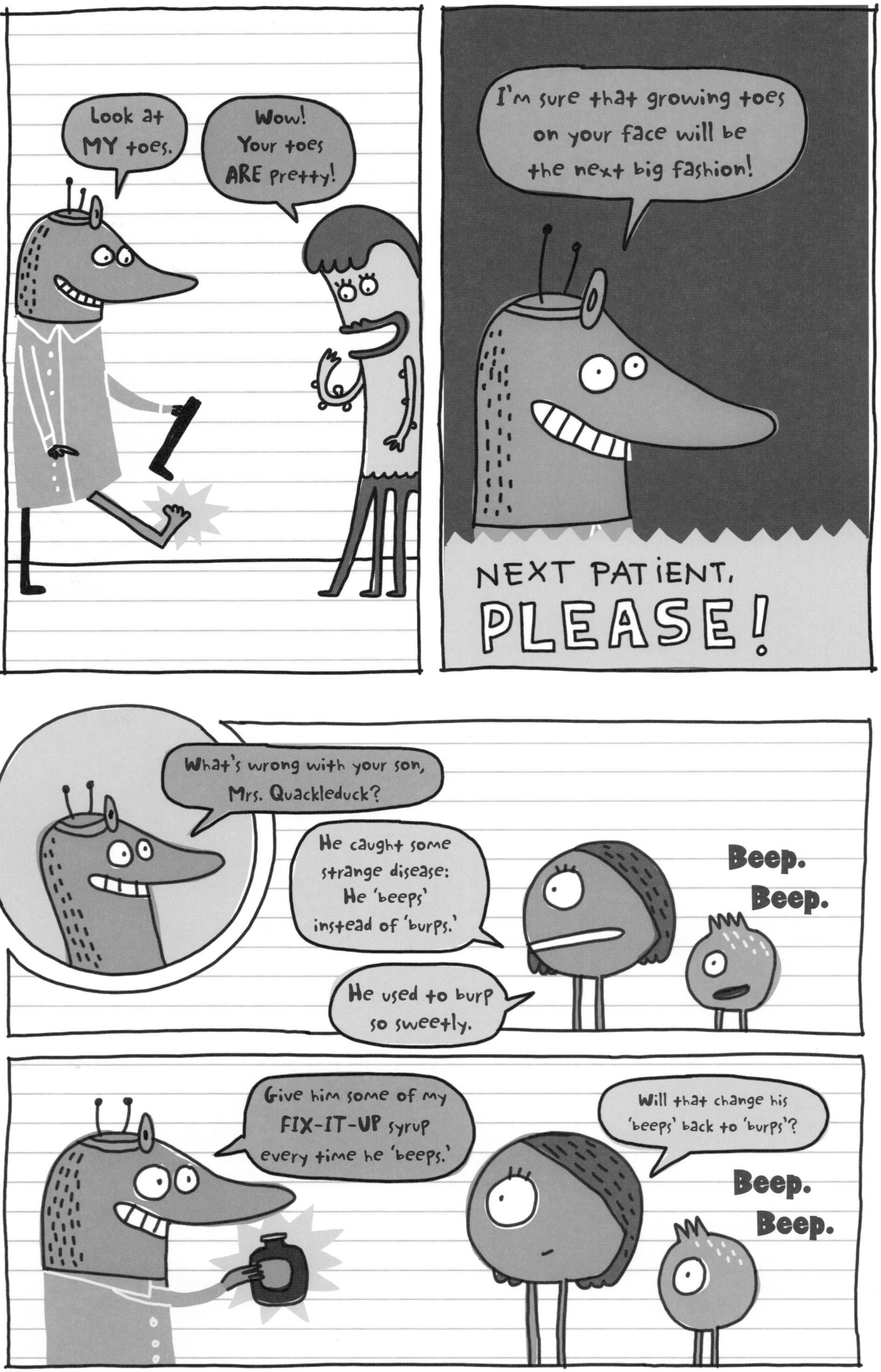
Look at MY toes.
Wow! Your toes ARE pretty!
I'm sure that growing toes on your face will be the next big fashion!
NEXT PATIENT, PLEASE!
What's wrong with your son, Mrs. Quackleduck?
He caught some strange disease: He 'beeps' instead of 'burps.'
He used to burp so sweetly.
Beep. Beep.
Give him some of my FIX-IT-UP syrup every time he 'beeps.'
Will that change his 'beeps' back to 'burps'?
Beep. Beep.